The Slickrock Cafe

· F O R ·

Mindy

CHAPTER 1

Bud Shumway rubbed his earlobe a bit as he steered his big John Deere 5415 tractor, cruising in a big semicircle around the edge of the watermelon field he was working. The lobe still tingled now and then, and he was having trouble getting used to the little silver knob that poked out from it.

He wondered what his daddy, who'd been a tough uranium miner all his life, would think of Bud getting his ear pierced. He probably wouldn't have approved, thought Bud, and was maybe even rolling over in his grave right now. As for his momma, she probably would've thought it was great, she being the source of the occasional liberal thoughts that kept Bud awake at night in a state of cognitive dissonance.

Bud was sure his grandpa, who'd been sheriff up in Carbon County, wouldn't have approved. In fact, Bud himself had been sheriff here in Emery County not so long ago, and he knew this act would save him from ever being considered for that office again—not that he wanted it.

Bud turned the wheels and straightened out the tractor. It was fall, and he was preparing the soil for the winter, plowing under the melons that hadn't made it to market for various reasons. They were few and far between, as the

Krider Melon Farm had seen a successful harvest, which made both Bud and his boss, Bill Krider, very happy. It was the first season for them both, Krider just recently deciding to add farming to his list of accomplishments, which included being a well-known mystery writer.

Now Bud's ear was starting to itch a bit. He wondered if he'd had the correct ear pierced, as he knew there was an unspoken language of such—right meant you were gay, or was it left? Maybe he should get the other pierced, too, but he wasn't sure if that maybe meant you were bisexual or something. The woman who'd done the piercing up in Price had just laughed when he'd asked. She said it just didn't matter anymore, as everyone was doing it. Bud sure hoped she was right.

It had all been his wife Wilma Jean's idea. She had told Bud she was sick and tired of him always fiddling with something, and it drove her crazy. First it had been the Dentine gum, then rubbing the bridge of his nose, then his sunglasses, which he was always losing, which made him then revert again to rubbing the bridge of his nose. Maybe, just maybe, if he had something kind of embarrassing to fiddle with, he'd get over the habit. He could eventually let the piercing grow back when he was cured.

Bud reminded her that he fiddled because he was a thinker. Besides, it was better than him smoking, wasn't it? Wilma Jean agreed, but she still wanted to try out her theory. Bud then reminded her that a guy having his ear pierced was actually considered cool in some parts of the country. She had in turn reminded him that this was Green River, Utah, not New York City.

In the end, Bud had complied, even if against his better senses, letting Wilma Jean drive him the 65 miles to

Price, to the nearest beauty salon, which was embarrassing enough in itself to enter.

He was surprised to see a couple of guys getting haircuts and wondered what happened to the good old barbershop days. Since Wilma Jean always cut his hair, he was obviously out of touch.

And now, sure enough, as he thought about all this, Bud was now starting to fiddle with the ear-post—or whatever the hell the thing was called. He had put his foot down when the beautician had wanted to put a nice big silver hoop in his ear—he told her it might interfere with his farming. For some reason, this had elicited a big smile on her part, as well as from the two guys getting their hair cut. Bud had kind of slinked out, leaving Wilma Jean to pay the bill.

Bud stopped the tractor to take out the alcohol and cotton he was supposed to use when the lobe started itching, but just then his cell phone rang. He looked at the caller ID but didn't recognize the number. He could tell from the prefix, however, that it was someone down in his old hometown of Radium.

He wondered how his old law-enforcement buddies down there would take his new fashion statement. He thought of his old friend, Humboldt "Hum" Stocks, who was sheriff there. Maybe word on Bud's progressiveness had gotten out, and they wanted him to come be under-sheriff, he mused.

He had no idea how close to being right he was.

• • •

Bud's dad had always said "Jell-low" when he answered the phone, but Bud had improved on it a bit, now that he was no longer sheriff and supposed to be formal.

"Yell-low," he answered.

For a bit, all he could hear was someone sobbing, then a woman's voice said, "Is this Bud, Bud Shumway?"

Bud answered, "It is."

"Bud, this is Peggy Sue Stocks, you know, Hum's wife."

"Peggy Sue! I sure haven't heard from you guys for a bit. How's Hum? Is everything OK?"

He heard more sobbing, then Peggy Sue answered, "No, Bud, Hum went into the hospital, and they say he might not come back out. Bud, we really need you down here, can you come right away?"

"Well, of course, Peggy Sue, but what's going on?"

"Bud, they're saying Hum was attacked. He has a head injury, and I think someone tried to kill him. He was investigating a murder. Please, Bud, can you come right now? Please?"

"I'll be right there," Bud answered, hanging up the phone just as an old Buddy Holly tune started up in his mind—"I love you, Peggy Sue..."

He wondered who had been murdered. He grimaced a bit—he was wishing right there and then he had waited a day or two to get his ear pierced. Now everyone in Radium would know.

CHAPTER 2

Bud parked the tractor at the edge of the field where his 1975 Toyota FJ40 waited. He'd bought it just a month ago, and even though it was used, it was his pride and joy. He'd had his buddy Derrill at Cosmic Collision give it a new paint job—it was now Sandstorm Tan instead of Grenade Green—and Wilma Jean was helping him refurbish the interior with matching tan cloth on the seats, though they had a ways to go, having just now picked out the cloth.

When Wilma Jean got involved, things often took unpredicted turns, and this had been no different, with her driving over to Grand Junction, Colorado to find the right material, which ended up having safari lions and tigers in the print. Bud knew he would take a ribbing from his buddies for that, but he didn't care. Everything Wilma Jean did had panache, and that fortunately included her cooking.

Bud checked his watch—2 p.m. He hoped he'd get back in time for dinner tonight, as Wilma Jean was making pork chops stuffed with apples from their own tree, and he sure didn't want to miss that. It would take an hour to get to Radium, then another hour to get home, so if he stayed only an hour or two, he had a good chance of hitting it just right—right out of the oven.

He stopped by their bungalow, just down the road a bit from the farm, where he grabbed a few things—his warm jacket, a cold soda, and his almost empty wallet—he might want a cup of hot coffee on his way home. He noted that Hoppie and Pierre, their dogs, were gone, as was Wilma Jean and her hot pink Lincoln Continental.

She must be taking the dogs for a ride, Bud thought. He was home early, so she wouldn't be expecting him. He wondered if she'd already started on the pork chops. He opened the refrigerator door. On the top shelf was an apple pie, probably for dinner, he figured, and he grabbed a slice and headed out the door.

Just as he closed the door and walked out onto the porch, he paused, then turned and went back into the house, took his Ruger revolver and shoulder holster from the gun safe, grabbed some ammo, then turned and went back out, pie in one hand and gun in the other.

• • •

As Bud cruised through the little desert town of Green River, he kept an eye out for Wilma Jean, but he never did see her. She wasn't at the Melon Rind Cafe, nor was she at the bowling alley, both businesses she owned. He stopped at the Eastwinds Truck Stop and topped off his gas tank, even though it was only 50 miles or so to Radium. It was a habit he'd gotten into when he was sheriff. Never know where you might end up.

He finally headed out and crossed the bridge over the river, noting that the nearby Krider Melon Farms produce stand was still doing a brisk business, even though it was the end of the season. Professor Krider had hired his two girls, who had recently graduated from high school, to run it. They'd turned out to be marketing gurus, putting up handmade signs along the highway, even though Bud thought it might be of questionable legality.

But Green Riverites were typically free thinkers, and this by default made them take things into their own hands, especially when it came to what they considered meaningless laws made at the state level. Besides, the signs were of the old Burma Shave variety, and everyone enjoyed them.

Bud cruised on out over the railroad bridge, kind of half watching for a train to come by, when he suddenly noted something different behind him—red lights flashing. He hadn't been paying attention to the speed limit, but then, in Green River, nobody did. Everyone drove too slow to worry about getting a speeding ticket—except tourists. He pulled over, and the red lights went off.

Must be Howie, he mused, his former deputy who had become sheriff when Bud resigned. A state trooper would have left the lights flashing.

Sure enough, a tall lanky guy in the khaki uniform of the Emery County Sheriff's Office emerged from a brand-new Forest Green Toyota Land Cruiser and walked up to Bud's window.

"Howdy, Sheriff," he addressed Bud. "You're under arrest for going too slow."

Bud grinned. "Howie, when are you gonna quit calling me sheriff? I haven't been sheriff for four months now."

Bud opened his door and got out, shaking Howie's hand. They both leaned against Bud's vehicle.

"Sorry, Bud. But right about now I'm wishing you were sheriff. Sorry about pulling you over like that, but I need your help."

Bud was beginning to understand how a preacher must feel—everyone needs your help, and usually you couldn't do anything.

"Howie, why didn't you just call me on my cell phone like you usually do instead of pulling me over?"

"I can't find it, Sheriff. Besides, I kind of want to talk to you in person about this."

Howie hadn't changed a bit, Bud noted, always making him explore all over for clues to the mystery du jour. Bud usually felt like he needed a metal detector to even get close.

"What's up? Does it have to do with being sheriff?" Bud asked.

"No, that's OK, I'm doing way better there than I thought I would, thanks to all your advice, which I really do appreciate, Bud, and I hate to always bother you like I do. I sure quit worrying and settled down after you left me."

"Sounds like the words to a country-western song, Howie."

Howie chuckled. "Yeah, it does, doesn't it? But this has to do with my ex-wife, Maureen. I just got a call from her."

"I thought you lost your cell phone, Howie."

"I did, but after the call. Actually, that's why I lost it, cause I was so discombobulated. Sheriff, I really need your advice. I can see you're on the road to somewhere, but I couldn't help it. I was about ready to go out to Krider's and look for you, so I'm glad I caught you. I know it's probably illegal to pull you over like this, but I didn't figure you'd arrest me or anything." Howie grinned.

"It's OK, Howie. What's up with Maureen?"

"I dunno. You know, we've been divorced about two years now, and she's been dating other guys, and now she says she wants us to get back together again. Man, that hit me out of left field."

"Well, that would sure make it easier on you when they move the sheriff's office over to Castle Dale, wouldn't it?"

"Well, not really, cause she says she hates it over there and wants to come back to Green River. I don't know what to do, Bud. If I weren't sheriff, I could just be running my little drive-in and she could help me, like we used to do."

"Did the new owner ever get caught up on his payments?" Bud asked.

"No, he's now seven months behind. He's ruining that place, I swear, Bud. I sit there across the street and watch it go further downhill every day, like an out-of-control 18-wheeler coming down that steep grade at Spotted Wolf."

"Well, Howie, it's pretty much your call. But if you still love Maureen and want to get back together, why not take the place back and let her run it? That way you can still be sheriff—you guys will just be across the street from each other. And when they move the office, you can go back to running the cafe like before."

"Bud, you're a very smart man, did anyone ever tell you that?" Howie beamed.

"Would you do me a favor and tell that to Wilma Jean?" Bud joked. "But Howie, I gotta run down to Radium. Sheriff Hum's in the hospital. He was covering a murder, and it appears maybe he was attacked, though nobody knows for sure. I may need your help if things get crazy, so stand by." Bud paused, kind of amazed at the words coming out of his mouth.

"Roger and 10-4," Howie replied. "It would be an honor to help out any way I can. I miss working with you, Sheriff. Say, what's up with your ear there, if I might ask?"

"Nothing much," Bud said, getting back into his FJ. "Just a little present from Wilma Jean." He grinned, touched his hat brim in salute, and headed out to the freeway, again fidgeting with the earlobe and thinking back to his time as Sheriff of Emery County.

Once again, he felt gratitude to Professor Krider for his new job—Bud loved being a peaceful melon farmer and didn't miss being sheriff one bit.

CHAPTER 3

Bud cruised down the freeway, watching his speed, which wasn't hard to do in his FJ, as it started to rattle when he broke 60. He started to see some of the signs the girls had made.

Feeling hungry?
Thirsty, too?
Try Krider's Melons
And Honeydew.

He smiled. His first season at Krider's had been a resounding success, and once he got the fields ready for next spring, he would pretty much have the winter off. He looked forward to spending more time with Wilma Jean, helping in the cafe and bowling alley—or catching up on his reading at home, with their Bassett hound, Hoppie, and their dachshund, Pierre, at his feet, or, more likely, the pair trying to squash into his big easy chair with him. He had a whole stack of Louis L'Amour paperbacks he wanted to get at. He might even try his hand at a little cooking and help Wilma Jean out.

Got a headache?
Toothache, too?

11

Krider's Melons
Good for you.

Now Bud's earlobe was itching again, and he realized he hadn't brought the alcohol and cotton with him. He fiddled with the silver ear-post with his left hand as he drove with his right. He noticed a small herd of antelope standing on a hill near the freeway, where they appeared to be watching the traffic.

Bud loved this vast open high desert of Mancos shale, something very few people could understand, he supposed. But it had to do with long and wide open spaces with no people, and the freedom to go wherever you could get yourself to. He liked that. Plus, the sunsets were usually fantastic, and you could even see the green flash once in awhile, that rare chromatic aberration that one could see only on wide horizons. Maybe he'd get a good camera and take up photography, he mused. Maybe a Canon—they had a good reputation and were affordable. He'd have to check out the prices.

Hubby says
You're getting fat?
Try Krider's Melons,
Good for that.

Bud was getting close to the Radium exit when he saw Amtrak. The silver train wound its sinuous way along the distant Bookcliffs, which formed an imposing backdrop of high blue-gray cliffs. He wished he had that camera right now, and a good telephoto lens to go with it. He was starting to look at things like a photographer would, framing them and all that. Bud thought he might make a darn good photographer, come to think of it.

Wifey says
You're obese?
Eat Krider's Melons
And cut the grease.

Bud took the exit for Radium just as the train wound out of sight, heading west, on its way to Green River. It then struck him that the train was either four hours early or about twenty hours late, as it usually left Green River going west around six p.m.

More likely late, he figured, though this might be setting a record for tardiness, even for them. He kind of wished he were on it, going somewhere new to some exciting adventure. But then, he'd miss Wilma Jean and the kids, Pierre and Hoppie. Maybe going somewhere new for just a few days, he decided.

He was now heading south on the highway towards the town of Radium, the freeway behind. He could see the red cliffs that surrounded the town in the far distance. The beautiful Salt Mountains stood above the redrock cliffs, forming a perfect backdrop of blue and white, an early snowfall lighting up the peaks.

His cell phone rang. It was Wilma Jean.

"Hon, you need to get home right now, we've had a burglary," she said. "Where are you, anyway? I drove out to the farm, but you're not there."

Bud wasn't sure what to say. Finally, he asked, "You must've come in the south end as I was going out the north. What was stolen?"

Wilma Jean laughed. "A nice big slice of the pie I was going to take to the library meeting tonight. Vanished into thin air. Nary a clue."

Bud relaxed. "You have to forgive the thief when you have stuff like that around. Too tempting. I'm sorry, Hon."

Wilma Jean laughed. "It's OK, I'll get a cheesecake at the store. You can have more pie with your dinner tonight, which I won't be attending because of the meeting. Where are you?"

Bud replied, "You're still making pork chops, aren't you? Mashed potatoes would be good with that, you know. I'm on my way to Radium, but I'll be back for dinner. Hum's in the hospital."

"That's too bad. Is that Peggy Sue's Hum?"

"Yeah, she called and asked me to come down this afternoon." Bud almost added "to help check out a murder," but he decided it wouldn't be wise, as he had no such intention and didn't want to worry his wife. He would see Hum and Peggy Sue and then go home. The Radium Sheriff's Office could deal with what was going on well enough, they were a competent bunch.

"Well, OK," replied Wilma Jean, "But I'd better not leave it in the oven in case you're late. You'll have to warm it up yourself. Drive safe."

With that, Wilma Jean was gone, just in time for Bud to hang up and drive, as what appeared to be some kind of motorcycle gang passed him. He could barely read the back of one of the jackets, they were going so fast, but it appeared to say, "Minot Marauders." Probably a bunch of bankers and lawyers out on a lark, he thought, wondering if any of them had pierced ears.

• • •

Bud pulled up in front of Radium Memorial Hospital, the site of his own birth. He'd always wondered how his momma ended up here, as his parents were living over in Hanksville at the time, where his daddy was a uranium miner in the Temple Mountain district. He always figured it was because there was no hospital in Hanksville—there wasn't much of anything in Hanksville.

The family had moved to Radium shortly thereafter when his dad started mining out north on the Poison Strip. Bud had always kind of wished he'd been born in the back of his daddy's big blue Thunderbird, over in Hanksville. It had more mystique and would explain the wanderlust that hit him from time to time. But he was sure his mom had preferred Radium Memorial, and his daddy had never even owned a Thunderbird, just an old Dodge Power Wagon. Being born in the back of an old Dodge Power Wagon just wouldn't have been the same.

Bud walked in the front doors, looking around for someone to help him, but the hospital was too small to have a receptionist—either that or she was missing in action—so he just wandered around a bit until he found a nurse, who directed him to Hum's room.

Peggy Sue was sitting by Hum's bed, holding his limp hand, while Hum appeared to be sleeping. Her eyes were swollen and red, matching her bright red hair. She was petite and slim and wore blue jeans and an oversized plaid men's shirt, the long shirttail tied into a knot on one side of her hips. She wore sneakers with no socks and her hair was tied into a ponytail.

Bud hadn't seen Peg and Hum for a good few years, but she hadn't changed a bit. In fact, Bud thought, she hadn't changed a bit since they were all in high school together. Bud had always thought that she looked to be straight out of the 50s. Maybe there was a reason she always reminded him of that Buddy Holly song.

Bud quietly approached the bed, kind of leaning over Hum, who had an IV going into the arm that Peg wasn't holding. Various monitors were attached to his heart, and his head was wrapped in bandages.

"Hi, Hum," he said. "Hi, Peg. How's it going?"

"Oh-my-go-to-heck, it's Bud! You did come, just like you said you would. Hum, Bud's here."

There was no sign of recognition from Hum. In fact, there was no sign of anything, and Bud wondered if he were even breathing. A light movement in Hum's chest region indicated he was, as well as an EKG monitor that said his heart was beating.

Bud sat down in a chair. "What's going on, Peg?"

Peggy Sue let go of Hum's hand and leaned back, sighing, looking like she was about to cry again.

"He called in a 911 on his cell phone yesterday afternoon, then nothing else was heard from him. All he said was, 'I need medical assistance.' They used the GPS on the phone to track him up above town, out in the rocks. By then, he was unconscious. He hasn't woke up since they found him, and the doctor says it's a severe concussion."

"You said something about a murder. What's that all about? Do you think this is related?"

"Oh yes, I do! Hum had been investigating the murder of Jimmy Ottin, you know, the guy who has the rock shop. Funny thing, Bud, Jimmy was killed up above town in the rocks. I know it's related. Hum went out there to look around, and this is how he came back." She started silently sobbing.

"How long you been here, Peg? Maybe you should go home. I can sit with him for a bit. I'd like to, actually, and I want to talk to his doctor. Why don't you run on home and get some rest. You look pretty haggard."

Peggy Sue stopped sobbing. "Yes, I need to, I've been here almost 24 hours. But what if I leave and he..."

Bud replied, "It's OK, Peg. He's just as likely to wake up as not. Sometimes concussions are like a big binge, you need to sleep them off. You go get some rest and you can always call me to see how he's doing. I'll call you if anything changes."

Peggy Sue was soon gone, and Bud kicked back, thinking of a concussion he'd received not all that long ago while investigating his last case, the one that led to him quitting the Sheriff's Department. He hoped to never go through that again—it was a real pain.

His ear was itching again, so he looked around a bit in the cupboards for some alcohol. Sure enough, he found some and splashed it around the ear-post. That helped, and he sat back down and watched for any signs of change from Hum.

Nothing. He sat for a bit, then started getting sleepy. The room seemed too hot, so he cracked open the window, letting in some fresh air, then sat back down. He started talking, mostly to keep himself awake.

"Hum, you remember that time in high school we painted over the big R up on the cliffs? Man, that was something. You guys let me down on a rope and I covered the whole thing up with brown paint. The whole town was in an uproar and thought the Green River football team had done it." He laughed, thinking back. He and Hum went way back to when they were kids.

"Hows about that time we had the double date at the drive-in? You and that little Kissel gal and me and Wilma Jean. She thought you were getting a bit fresh there in the backseat and knocked you out cold. She couldn't have been more than five feet tall. What a pistol." Bud laughed. "See, this isn't the first time you've been out cold. You'll recover." He thought he detected a bit of movement in Hum's cheek, but wasn't sure.

"Say, Hum, remember when your dad was mayor and declared Radium to be a United Nations-free zone? If you were in the U.N., you couldn't come into the county, not that anybody from the U.N. even knew Radium existed. That was a crackup, for sure. We all laughed hard over that one, except for the one or two liberals in town. And hows about when he tried to get a resolution passed that you had to carry a gun if you were over 18? Everyone in Radium, man and woman alike, would be required to carry a gun. He said it was required by the Constitution. Got a little national press over that one." Now Bud was quiet, wondering what had really happened to Hum. He decided to go find the doctor, but was soon back, as the doc was nowhere to be found.

He leaned again over Hum's bed, noting the drawn look, his pale skin, how Hum's square cheekbones seemed to stand out even more than usual. He noticed Hum seemed to be going a bit gray.

Bud then leaned down and whispered conspiratorially in Hum's ear.

"Hum, I hate to tell you this, but Wilma Jean made me get my ear pierced."

To Bud's surprise, Hum's eyes opened wide, and he began to mumble.

CHAPTER 4

Bud couldn't believe it! Hum was leaning up on his elbow, talking incoherently. He didn't know whether to go for the nurse or to stay and listen.

He decided to listen. He needed to ask Hum some questions.

Hum was actually whispering more than talking, and Bud had to lean over him to make out what he was saying. Bud wanted hard to capture every word and now wished he'd brought the little pocket recorder he had carried when he was sheriff.

Hum mumbled, "Bud, make sure Peggy Sue's looked after, won't you? Promise me?"

Bud wasn't sure what all that might entail, but he promised, then assured Hum he would soon be fine and able to do it himself.

Hum continued. "Bud, my head hurts...so groggy..."

Bud waited, hoping Hum would stay awake.

Hum continued, "It's all because of them Malachites, Bud. You need to get them Malachites out of there—take them to the museum or something. They're bad news. Jimmy was fighting somebody over them up at the Slick-rock Cafe and they killed him. He was a good man. And that Black Beast, it's not...I'm so groggy..."

As suddenly as he'd awakened and started talking, Hum slipped back onto his pillow and into a deep sleep.

Bud had wanted to ask Hum what the Malachites were and where the Slickrock Cafe was and what this Black Beast was, but it was too late, so instead, he went and got the nurse.

• • •

Hum's nurse had run Bud out, saying since he wasn't family he couldn't be there with Hum in such critical condition. He had wanted to call Peggy Sue, but decided not to, as she needed to rest, and he knew she would just come back down to the hospital.

Instead, he called Wilma Jean's old friend Kathy, who was a nurse with the Radium Hospice. The hospital agreed to let her sit with Hum, as Bud knew Peg would never forgive him if he left Hum alone, even if he'd been given the boot and had no choice. Kathy promised to call both him and Peg if anything changed.

It was now going on evening, and as Bud left the hospital, he stood for a moment and watched the sun turn the redrock above town into a glowing backdrop. He'd forgotten how amazing it all was, how the redrock always glowed and looked like it was on fire when the sun went down. He sure needed to get that Canon and come back down here and do some photography soon, he thought.

He hoped Hum would be around to go out with him. Hell, maybe he could convince Hum to retire and take up photography, too, or at least get a less dangerous job, as Bud had done. Shoots, maybe Hum could get into film, that would really be something. In any case, he just wanted Hum to come back.

Bud decided to drive up above town and watch the sunset. He headed for the Dump Road, which wound above the town in a series of steep switchbacks, up into the red sandstone. His FJ chugged right up the road until he topped out high above town.

The views were spectacular, and he could now look down on the town, where lights were beginning to twinkle, although up here, the sun was still just above the rim on the far side of the valley. Radium set in a deep rift, with the Radium Rim on one side and the Slickrock Flats high above it on the other. It was all the result of a collapsed salt dome deep underneath which had taken the landscape with it millions of years ago, leaving a huge canyon and also a number of underground caves beneath the town.

Bud chugged on past the dump, noting the sign that designated it as the World's Most Scenic Dump. He wondered who had done the designating. Whoever it was, they had to be right, as the dump itself set on a tilted hill with the Salt Mountains as a backdrop, along with huge redrock fins marching in a line to the base of a huge red mesa that fronted the snow-covered mountains.

It was like being in a landscape painting, he thought, except for the dump part. He wished he had that Canon right now, cause the oblique angle of the sun had lit the fins so they looked like they were burning.

He was now climbing another steep switchback that would top out at Slickrock Flats, which had nothing flat about it at all. In fact, it was a wonderland of huge slickrock fins and slot canyons and rounded domes called whale-backs that went on for miles and miles. The only thing that kept one from being able to hike all the way from the road on into the dinosaur bone lands north of town was Granstaff Canyon, where a creek had gradually cut through the rock, eventually forming a large canyon system. Up high here, he could look down on the tops of the canyon walls in the distance, draped with shining black desert varnish.

The road now flattened out, and Bud could see the unbelievable landscape of the Slickrock Flats all around him. Radium was no longer visible, lying far below. He went through a narrow passage between two huge fins, then pulled the FJ over by another huge fin called the Arrowhead. He got out and set on a big rock.

He had practically grown up here, and everywhere he turned there were memories. He studied a distant stock trail that wound down into the fins then back up and around on a big flat hill, then dropped down again, and he could have described about every foot of it, he'd been on it so many times—on horseback, in an ATV, on a dirt bike, hiking, and he'd even mountain biked it a few dozen times.

In fact, when he'd been involved in the uranium mine cave-in that ended his mining career here, he'd lain in a hospital bed and hiked that road many times in his mind. It had been about the only thing that kept him going through all that, hoping to get out to the slickrock again. That and Wilma Jean.

The sun had now gone down enough that it began lighting the flanks of the Salt Mountains high above. They were the most photogenic mountains in the world, he thought—at least in his world. There were three different subranges, all close together, and the sun lit up some peaks, then others, in a show of light that Bud had seen many times but that always amazed him.

The snow turned gold, then red, then purple with al-penglow as the sun moved further and further down the horizon, and now Bud wasn't sure which way to look, as sunrays caught a bit of cloud above Radium and turned it into a kaleidoscope of color as the alpenglow deepened.

He wished Wilma Jean were here to watch it with him—it seemed selfish to be the only one enjoying this. He also wished Hum were here, all better and happy again—and Peggy Sue. They could all have a big picnic, with stuffed pork chops. Bud wondered if this would end Hum's career as a lawman, assuming he recovered enough to do any-thing. He wondered again where and what the Slickrock Cafe was, then started thinking about dinner. He should head back to Green River soon.

Then, just as suddenly as that, the sunset was over, except for the purple shadows that lingered. Now the fins and whalebacks took on a more ominous aspect, and Bud recalled many times being out here at night and how it sometimes made him feel unsettled, as opposed to being north of town in the dino-bone country, which was open and felt safe. He never really did understand why he had never enjoyed camping here that much, as it was his fa-vorite landscape in the daylight. But there was something about these big fins at night—they were mysterious, and about anything could be hiding between them.

A lone coyote started yipping, then suddenly stopped. Bud turned one last time to look at the distant trail, and he thought he saw movement about a quarter-mile out. The shadows were lengthening. He got his binoculars from the FJ—if someone was out there, maybe it had something to do with Hum and all that, and he wanted to see what it was.

He could barely see anything, as the dark was falling fast—but wait—there, he'd managed to almost focus on it. Whatever it was, it was moving along at a good clip, yet it didn't seem to be a vehicle. Maybe a dirt biker, he thought, but surely he would hear it, as dirt bikes were so noisy. And it didn't have a headlight—or dust trail.

As Bud watched, he noted that whatever it was, it was coming his way, and fast. He began to feel uneasy, his sixth sense warning him that maybe things weren't right. It was a feeling he had learned to listen to during his five years as sheriff, and it had served him well.

In fact, this feeling was what had saved his life even before that, when he was a miner. During the mine cave-in, he'd started running before he even knew what was going on—something told him to run, and when the others saw him, they ran too and no one had been killed, though he and three others were injured. He'd received a commendation from the Governor. He never dreamed he'd get commended for running like a madman and yelling at the top of his lungs, scared to death.

Now he could finally begin to make out what this thing was, and he didn't like what he saw one bit. It appeared to be some kind of animal, and it looked to be as black as tar. And it was now only maybe a couple of tenths of a mile away, moving fast.

Bud put his hand into his jacket, making sure his Ruger was ready, then put the binoculars back up to his eyes. In that short time, the thing had made remarkable time towards him, and was now only a mere tenth of a mile away. Yet he still couldn't make out exactly what it was, as he couldn't quite seem to focus on it. It now went behind a small grove of juniper trees and seemed to have disappeared, yet Bud knew there were lots of ways for it to continue and still be hidden. It could now be coming up a small wash not far away.

Feeling panicked, Bud jumped into the FJ, started up and took off. He wished later he had stayed and seen for himself what the thing actually was, but at the time, the ungodly scream that cut through the air around him made him want to do nothing but flee, which he did, stopping only when, an hour later, he reached his bungalow at the edge of Green River.

Somehow he knew he had met Hum's Black Beast.

CHAPTER 5

The next day, Bud sat kicked back in his big easy chair, Hoppie sleeping at his feet and Pierre somehow snugged down between Bud and the arm of the chair in one of those maneuvers only long skinny weener dogs can do. Every once in awhile the little black and tan dog would kick his little legs and start barking.

Bud leaned down and whispered softly, "Get 'em, Pierre, get the wabbits." The little dog's legs kicked harder, like he was running, until he finally woke himself up. He had also woken Hoppie up, and now both sat and watched Bud, hoping he'd decide to go get a snack or something.

Bud put down the Bible he'd been reading, then went into the kitchen and made himself a plate of leftover pork chops and mashed potatoes. Hoppie and Pierre would get the bones. They'd apparently been able to effectively tele-path their wishes to him—but then, it was a ritual they all participated in every day at lunchtime.

Bud had been back out at Krider's all morning, finishing up the fields, and he was now taking a lunch break before going back out. He was as close to being done out there as you could get, and he figured he'd be finished in a couple of hours. At that point, all that was left to do all winter long was some equipment maintenance, and he could do that about anytime.

But right now, he wanted to see where in the Bible it mentioned the Malachites. He knew he'd seen it in there somewhere, and he wanted to find it, see if it would help him figure out what Hum had said at the hospital yesterday.

He sat back down in his easy chair, balancing his plate on one leg and the Bible on the other, the dogs devotedly watching him eat. He and Wilma Jean weren't particularly religious, and it had been a long time since he'd read the Bible.

He kept getting sidetracked by some of the stories, like asses that talked (he'd met a few himself), pillars of light (which he'd seen a few times as the sun set), and such. He was particularly intrigued by the mention of people turning into salt and wished he could figure out how that was done—that and the water into wine trick would be great party jokes. He frowned, feeling a bit sacrilegious.

But he still had to find mention of any Malachites. He was sure he'd read about the Israelites fighting them or something somewhere. He'd have to ask Pastor Wilkins down at the Community Bible Church—he would know.

Bud threw the dogs the bones, having left a few bites of meat on each, and put his plate in the dishwasher. He needed to get back out to the fields and finish up. Professor Krider had been gone to a mystery writer's convention in New York, but he should be back sometime today, and Bud wanted to have everything tied up. But he'd first make a cup of coffee and see about those Malachites.

The little espresso machine hissed and boiled until finally a black brew came dripping out, Bud's version of coffee, though it was closer to the dictionary definition of mud. Bud put a big dollop of vanilla bean ice cream in it and sat back down.

Just then his cell phone rang, interrupting any further Bible studies.

"Yell-ow," Bud answered.

"Hey Bud, Bill Krider here. I'm back. How's everything going?"

"Just great, Prof. Almost done. As soon as I finish this coffee, I'm heading back out. How was the conference?"

"Super. Really enjoyed it and met a few old friends. Say, I'm close to your place, mind if I stop by?"

"Of course not," Bud replied. "In fact, I may have some grist for a new book, wouldn't mind running some things by you."

"No kidding? I'll be right there."

"No need to knock, just come on in," Bud answered.

• • •

Professor Krider was soon there, and the dogs greeted him as he came in the kitchen door and on into the living room, where Bud sat.

Noting the Bible, the Prof said, "I didn't realize you were a religious man, Bud."

Bud laughed. "Yeah, when you hear me cussin' that tractor, you sure wouldn't guess it, would you? Maybe put a 'sac' in front of 'religious.'"

Krider grinned. "Learning anything?"

"Nah, I'm trying to figure out where the Malachites come into the picture."

"The Malachites? Aren't they that country next to the Azurites? Or was that the Smectites?" Krider continued to grin. "And exactly what picture is that?"

Bud sat there, feeling kind of like a fool.

He replied, "It's a mineral, dang it, I knew that. If it had been a snake it would've bit me. Hum and me used to hang out at the Blue Jay Pit, a malachite-azurite mine there out of Radium. Our buddy, Charlie, his family runs it."

"Well, yes, last I heard it was a mineral. But you weren't that far off. They supposedly mined malachite at King Solomon's Mines. But why the interest? You going prospecting this winter?" Krider asked.

Bud stood up and put the Bible back into the bookcase. "Prof, there's been a murder down in Radium. I went down there yesterday afternoon to see my old friend, Sheriff Hum Stocks, who was hit in the head and is now in a deep sleep. He woke up just long enough to mention something about the Malachites. I'm sure worried about him, and I don't know how to go about helping him, but I want to see justice done."

"Bud, what about the guys down there, doesn't Radium have a good law-enforcement team?"

"Oh sure, they're fine. Hum was investigating the murder, and someone attacked him."

"What are you thinking about doing?"

"Well, as soon as I get that last field finished up, I'm thinking about going on back down there tomorrow, though I'm half scared of the place after last night—Slickrock Flats, that is."

He then told Krider about the Black Beast.

"Well, dang it, Bud, that sounds a lot like your last case to me, at least the Black Beast part. You have more guts than

I do. You know, I kind of hate seeing you go down there, it worries me. Call me selfish, but I'd hate to see anything happen to my farm manager."

"Call me selfish, too, then, cause I feel the same way," Bud replied.

"Bud, the reason I stopped is I want to share something with you."

With that, Krider pulled a newspaper clipping from his jacket pocket and handed it to Bud.

"Well, I'll be go-to-hell," Bud exclaimed. "No kidding? Mystery Writer's Book of the Year? I'll be darned."

Krider just grinned.

Bud added, "Hey, Prof, come help me solve a real mystery for once. You'd make a great partner. You can write about it. What say? 'The Mystery of the Black Beast'? 'Of the Malachites'? Or how about 'the Mystery of the Slickrock Cafe'?"

With that, Krider's face went a bit white. He sat down in the big overstuffed floral couch that Wilma Jean had bought at a yard sale up in Price. He slowly ran his hands through his graying hair, then stood back up and finally answered, "Bud, I appreciate the vote of confidence."

Bud thought Krider was about to decline, but the prof continued. "To help a lawman of your caliber would be a real honor. You know, I wouldn't miss it for anything. And that way I can make sure nothing happens to my farm manager. Tomorrow?"

"Tomorrow," Bud replied, noting the grin was back on Krider's face.

Krider then added, "And I don't mean to get personal, but just what the heck happened to your ear?"

CHAPTER 6

Bud had just pulled the meatloaf out of the oven when the call came. He later referred to it as "the Call," as if it were Divine Providence calling him back into law enforcement. After all, he'd been reading the Bible not long before, so maybe there was a connection, who could say?

In any case, it was a surprise, one that gave him the freedom and resources to investigate Hum's case as best he could and however he wanted.

"Yell-ow," Bud answered.

"Bud Shumway?"

"Depends on who's calling," Bud replied, grinning. He thought he recognized that voice.

"This is Earl, down in Radium, you remember me, Earl Talkington?"

"You bet, Earl, how could I forget a guy who was crazy enough to help me paint over the R? How's it going?"

"And to think we all went into law enforcement. Scary, ain't it?" Earl laughed, then added, "But speaking of law enforcement, Bud, you heard what happened to Hum Stocks?"

"I have. In fact, I was down there yesterday. I'm coming down tomorrow to see you guys and have a talk about it."

"So, somebody already told you the news?"

"What news?"

"That we want you to come down and act as Interim Sheriff until Hum gets better. You still farming, or you done for the winter?"

Bud was speechless for a moment.

"Would you repeat that, Earl?"

"I said, you done farming for the winter?"

"Yes, just finished today. No, the other part. You guys want me be Interim Sheriff? What about some of your own guys, they know the territory better than I do. Aren't you the second in command down there?"

"No offense to anyone, but Bud, nobody knows the country around here better than you do. As for me, I don't want the job. I'm retiring in a few days to start up my own radiator business. The mayor offered it to me and I turned him down, which didn't make him very happy, so it's a good thing I'm retiring. Of course, if I weren't retiring, I wouldn't have turned him down—it's all kind of circular. But anyway, what do you say? You'd make the same salary as Hum."

"How's he doing today, by the way? I was going to call his wife after dinner."

"The same. No change. We're all rootin' for him. One of us goes down there every day to talk to him, but so far, he ain't talkin' back."

"Is he still on salary?" Bud was thinking of his promise to look after Peggy Sue.

"He's on a medical leave of absence, and yes, the county still pays his salary."

"How long will they do that?"

"I think it's up to a year," Earl answered, "then something else kicks in, some long-term disability payment. But

Bud, why don't you call me in the morning? I know you'll want to talk to Wilma Jean about it. It would mean you moving down here for a bit, but we can help you with a house. We were all sad to hear you quit the sheriff's office up there, but now maybe we can get you down here for a bit, and it'll work out in our favor. The guys were 100% behind offering you the job."

"I'll have to sleep on it, Earl, but in any case, I'll be coming down your way tomorrow. Why don't I just stop in at the office there and give you my answer, say about mid-morning? Would that work?"

"You bet, Bud. Be good to see you."

• • •

Bud had put the meatloaf, baked potatoes, and salad on the table just as Wilma Jean drove up with Hoppie and Pierre. She hugged him as she walked in the door, sniffed a bit, then walked over to the table and gasped.

"Oh-my-gosh! I always wanted a real man, a man who could cook!" She laughed. "What's got into you?"

Bud stood there, beaming, then helped her with her jacket, hanging it on the hook on the back of the door.

"I told you when I got off for the winter I was going to start helping around here more. And I finished at Krider's early today, so here it is."

"It smells delicious," she said, sitting down at the table. "You know, cooking makes a man really attractive, but you know what's even more so?"

"What's that?" Bud asked, digging into the meatloaf. He hoped it had turned out OK, it being the first one he'd ever made.

"Having an earring. Pass the salad, please."

Wilma Jean smiled, then got up and kissed Bud on the forehead as she got the ketchup from the fridge.

They sat and ate awhile, Bud handing Hoppie and Pierre bites under the table, where he figured they pretended they were hounds in some Medieval castle, the way they kicked back and waited to be fed. Finally, he broke the silence.

"There's still some apple pie in the fridge. I'll heat you up a piece and put some ice cream on it when you're ready."

He knew Wilma Jean had already had a long day at the Melon Rind Cafe and would soon be off to the bowling alley for the evening. It would be his only chance to talk to her.

She looked at him suspiciously. "Did you do something you shouldn't have?"

He grinned. "No, nothing like what I'm about to do."

With that, he jumped up and went around to where she sat, pulling her from her chair and kissing her, meatloaf and all.

Hoppie started barking madly, while Pierre bit onto Bud's pant leg, growling and refusing to let go. Wilma Jean started laughing, and Bud began trying to gently shake the little dachshund off. The dog dragged along as Bud sat back down and wouldn't let go until Bud gave him a piece of meatloaf.

"I think Pierre likes trouble. Typical dachshund." Wilma Jean laughed. "But Hon, what's going on, really? I know you well enough to know something's bothering you."

"How can you tell that?" Bud asked.

"All you've done while we've been eating is fiddle with your ear. You've been getting really good about not fiddling, and here it comes again."

Bud suddenly got a sinking feeling. What would the guys down at Radium think about a sheriff with an earring? He wasn't so sure he would get the job after all. Oh well, if not, he would still go find out what happened to Hum and Jimmy Ottin.

"I got a call today from Earl, Hum's undersheriff. They want me to come down and be Interim Sheriff."

"I knew it." Wilma Jean put down her fork. Finally, she asked quietly, "Is that what you want to do?"

"Not really," he answered. "But it would make it easier for me to find out what happened to Hum. I was looking forward to having the winter here with you, helping out and relaxing and maybe even taking up some photography."

"Photography?" Wilma Jean looked surprised. "You haven't been interested in that since high school."

"I know. I haven't had the time to be interested in anything except work. That's the point. I've been looking at Canons, and I think I could really do some nice work, given the right equipment and time."

"Where would you stay, and how long would it last?"

"They said they'd get us a place in Radium, and it would last until Hum's better—could be a few weeks or awhile, but eventually, they'd have to get another real sheriff if he can't come back."

"What if that ended up being you?" Wilma Jean asked.

"Would you want to move back?" Bud asked.

"I dunno. After building up the cafe and bowling alley here...and all my friends...and I love this house, Bud. I don't know. But then, I really didn't want to leave Radium when we did, and that worked out."

"Well, we can take that fork when we come to it," Bud said. "In all honesty, I'm enjoying farming, and I'd hate to leave Krider in a bind after all he's done for me."

"Well, I think you should go ahead and take it for now," Wilma Jean said. "I know you want to. I'll come down on weekends, or you can come up here. And you can quit in the spring when Krider needs you. It wouldn't be the first time..."

Bud knew she was about to say, the first time they hadn't really been married. This was the main reason he'd quit law enforcement in the first place, as he never saw his wife. Maybe he shouldn't take the job. After all, he and Wilma Jean didn't really need the money, and he had been looking forward to having some free time. He and Krider could go down there on their own and investigate things.

"I've decided I'm not going to do it," he said.

Wilma Jean got up and put her dishes in the dishwasher.

"You take it," she said. "You owe it to Hum. I can come help out Peggy Sue. They're our friends, Bud, and they would do the same for us. I'll hire Krider's girls to help out with things here, they're smart as whips."

She put on her jacket. "I gotta get to the bowling alley, Hon. Thanks for dinner, it was great. But next time, don't use Ritz crackers, use regular saltines."

With that, she was out the door, tousling Bud's hair as she walked by, leaving Bud still sitting at the table, the dogs underneath, hoping for more.

Darn, Bud thought—he'd wondered why his meatloaf tasted different.

He dished the rest of the meatloaf onto two plates, gave it to the dogs, then went to clean up the kitchen, his hair standing straight up as if he'd seen the Black Beast itself.

CHAPTER 7

Bud and Professor Krider had left Green River after a cup
of coffee at the Chow Down and were well on their way
to Radium, almost to the freeway turnoff, when Bud's cell
phone rang.

"Yell-ow," Bud answered.

It was Howie.

"Sheriff, I got some real good news for you, and it's all
your doing."

Like a reluctant steer getting into a truck, Bud knew
Howie wouldn't move until prodded, so he replied, "What's
up, Howie?"

"Maureen's on her way to Green River with a moving
van. She's coming back!"

"That's great, Howie. Just great. I'm really happy for
you. Are you taking the cafe back?"

"Well, not yet. The new owner says he's gonna make up
all the back payments. I don't think he can do it, but I've
gotta give him a chance. I'm kind of worried about what
Maureen's gonna do, she's not the type to just sit around,
so I hope he can't pull it off, though I don't mean to sound
mean about it."

"That's just how business is, Howie. Say, why don't you
call Wilma Jean and see if she can put Maureen to work?

She was kind of relying on me to help her through the winter, but it looks like I'm going to be down in Radium for a bit."

"Radium?" Howie paused. "Say, Bud, can I still call you when I need to? Is it long distance down there?"

"Howie, it's a brave new world. Cell phones don't really care much about distance. You can call me anytime, you know that. Where'd you find it, anyway?"

"Find what, Bud?"

"Your phone.

"My phone? Oh, it was in the mike holder in the patrol vehicle."

"Where was the mike?"

"In my coat pocket. I hate these new wireless mikes."

Bud laughed. "Howie, I have some news for you. We're going to be colleagues again. I'm on my way down to Radium right now to accept the position of Interim Sheriff until Hum's better."

Bud watched Krider out of the corner of his eye to see how he would take the news.

Bud thought he could hear both Howie and Krider's jaws hitting the floor, but decided instead it was the siren behind him, complete with flashing red lights, signaling him to pull over.

This was getting to be a regular thing, he thought.

• • •

"Did I do anything wrong, Officer?" Bud asked the Radium County Deputy Sheriff who had just pulled him over. Bud didn't recognize him—must be one of the newer guys, he thought. The man's nametag read, "Deputy Hans Rohr."

"Can I see your license?" the deputy asked, blanching a little when he noticed Bud's silver ear-post.

Bud frowned, then pulled his license out of his wallet and asked again, "Did I do something wrong?" It was his constitutional right to know why he'd been pulled over, and he wanted to exercise that right.

Deputy Rohr answered, "You stay here. I'll be right back," then went and got into his dark blue Ford pickup with the sheriff's emblem on the side and light rack on top.

Krider looked at Bud. "He sure isn't going to tell you why he pulled you over, is he?"

Bud shrugged. "Guess not," he answered, fiddling with his ear-post, wishing now he'd had the other side done instead. He wondered if Hans had a dachshund and if mentioning Pierre would help things any.

Krider continued, "Boy, I can't wait to see his face when he finds out you're his new boss. You're going to be the new Radium sheriff, I take it, Bud?"

"Yeah, Prof, I'm accepting the job when we get down there today. They offered it to me last evening. I wanted to surprise you, cause I'm going to deputize you to help with this case, but it's probably better you know beforehand. You might not want to be a deputy when you see the way the Radium force abuses its power."

Bud added, "But it's just a short-term thing to help them out. I'm not quitting farming, but since we're done for the season, I figured it would be a good way to kill two birds with one stone—help Radium and also help us solve this case. In all honesty, Wilma Jean's a little miffed about it, but she told me to go ahead."

Just then, the deputy came back, returning Bud's license.

"Did you know you were going 50 in a 65 zone back there?"

Bud asked, "Is that illegal, Officer?"

Rohr answered testily, "No, Sir, it's not illegal, but you were holding up traffic. When you're going that slow, you need to pull over once in awhile so people can get around you."

"You're absolutely right," Bud answered measuredly. "I have a lot on my mind right now, but I'll be sure to do that from now on. You have a nice day, Officer."

Deputy Rohr got back into his vehicle and drove off. Bud and Krider both set there for a bit, amused, then Bud pulled back onto the highway.

"Did you notice I was leading a parade, Prof?" he asked.

"I saw two cars behind you. One was Deputy Rohr. I don't know if that qualifies as a parade or not."

Bud now noticed he'd forgotten to hang up his cell phone. "You still there, Howie?"

Howie answered, "Roger, still here, and I heard the whole thing. I can see the news now—Radium sheriff arrested for going too slow, just like I stopped you for the other day. You're gonna end up in prison if you don't change your ways, Sheriff." Howie snorted, then added, "10-4, over and out."

• • •

Bud leaned back in his new chair in his new office of Interim Sheriff of Radium County. It had been Earl's office, and was right next to Hum's office—which they were leaving be until Hum came back, though Bud had a key so he could access the files. Bud noted that his office had a good view of the clientele that came and went from the Uranium Diner across the street.

Mayor Ed Stocks, Hum's cousin, had sworn in both Bud and Bill during a quick ceremony. They would both soon be issued uniforms, but for now, Bud simply had a badge that declared him sheriff.

Krider sat across from Bud, fiddling with a badge that proclaimed him to be a deputy sheriff. He wore blue jeans with a tweed jacket over a t-shirt that read "Krider's Melons."

Krider said, "Bud, who would've guessed yesterday when I was over at your house that by today we'd both be LEO's?"

"Yesterday, I would've told you I'd never be a law-enforcement officer again, as long as I live," Bud replied.

"I wonder how the city of Radium feels about getting a bonus deputy," Krider said. "You suppose I'm on salary?"

"Believe it or not, you are," Bud answered. "But only part-time and temporary. I told them you came with the deal or no deal."

Just then someone tapped on the door's glass window.

"Come in," Bud said.

A short stocky man with red hair in a buzz cut and wearing a deputy sheriff's uniform entered. His nametag identified him as Deputy Calvin Murphy.

"Hey, Bud, nice to have you back in Radium. You wanted to see me?"

"Good to see you again, Cal. This is Deputy Bill Krider, he's new as of today, just part-time."

Krider stood and shook hands with Cal, looking amused.

Bud continued, "Cal, I need you to tell me everything you know about Jimmy Ottin's death. I understand you were the lead deputy that investigated it. And also anything you know about how Hum ended up in the hospital."

"You bet, Bud. I've been trying to follow up on things as best I can, but we've been shorthanded without Hum. Glad we're getting you and a new deputy, too. We could sure use the help." He nodded congenially towards Krider. "Mind if I sit down?" He scooted a chair over by the window and sat on it backwards, leaning back on two legs.

"Bud, you knew Jimmy. He's had that rock shop on the edge of town for years, and he's been in and out of trouble every year he's had it. First it was with the National Park Service for not getting a license to take tourists into the park. Then for driving tourists across Minuteman Arch in his old VW bus. Then every so often he'd get caught selling dinosaur bone in his shop, but we never could do anything as he said he collected on private lands and nobody could disprove it. Then he got into trouble for taking tourists into Arch Canyon after the BLM closed it off. All kinds of stuff, never a dull day around Jimmy. That's why everyone called him Jimmy Ought-not'n, instead of Jimmy Ottin."

"I remember," Bud replied. "I used to hang around his rock shop all the time when I was a kid. He and my dad were good friends. I grew up around Jimmy."

Cal put the chair legs down and grinned. "Yeah, wasn't he the one who masterminded painting over the R?"

"He was," Bud smiled. "And more besides that than most people will ever know. He was a character, one of a kind, born back when people were free thinkers. I always admired Jimmy."

"Well, I was one of those who got the honor of having to go tie his free thinking up a bit, so we butted heads a lot," Cal said.

"Who do you think murdered him? It was murder, wasn't it?"

"You bet it was murder, plain as day. Flat out shot in the back. No idea how long he lay out there on the rocks, dying, as a wound like that would take awhile to kill you. He bled to death. Nobody deserves to be shot in the back, that's a coward who would shoot like that. We found a casing and sent it to the ballistics lab, along with the bullet from his back."

"Any other marks?"

"No. He did have a handgun, and it had been discharged twice. I found one of the bullets lodged in a nearby pinion tree. I'll have Sandy bring over the coroner's report. She's our dispatcher and gofer gal."

"Thanks. Any idea who did it?" Bud asked.

"None at all, nor any idea why. I've been asking around town, talking to his friends, nobody knows why anyone would shoot a nice guy like Jimmy. Even as much as we butted heads, I still liked the guy. He'd try to buy me lunch every time he saw me, he always acted like I was a long-lost friend. He had a huge funeral, had people from all over the world there."

"Any clues around the murder scene?" Krider asked.

"Well, not really. You know how slickrock is—no footprints, nuthin'. We searched that whole area pretty damn good and didn't find a thing."

"Anyone besides you and the coroner know how Jimmy was killed?"

"No, that's top secret, though Hum knows, but he ain't talkin'. Even the hiker who found Jimmy didn't know, he just said he was passed out. It might be the one piece of evidence that helps solve the crime. We figure nobody but Jimmy and whoever else was there knows about that."

"Good. Where was he killed?" Bud asked.

"Kind of hard to describe...hell, you know Slickrock Flats better than anyone around here, so you'll know where I mean, with your photographic memory for places. You go up through Jack's Crack, then take a left there at the Arrowhead, that big rock. Then you have to park and start hiking. There's an old stock trail that winds down about a half-mile before it drops into Granstaff Canyon and goes down to the creek. Jimmy was killed right there, exactly before the trail starts down in there. There's a big old pinion tree right exactly where we found him. It's got a big porky scar on it."

"How long ago, and what about Hum?" Bud asked.

"Jimmy was killed a week ago today. As for Hum, we found him four days ago, a ways up the trail from where Jimmy was shot. There's a small ledge there. He has a cracked skull."

Cal stopped, then added solemnly, "Damn, Bud, I hope he gets better. I miss him. He was a damn good sheriff."

"He still is, and he'll be back, Cal, I just know it," Bud said softly.

Cal added, "Say, Bud, I forgot to mention one thing. Jimmy did have a blow to the head. The coroner said it's not what killed him, just a minor concussion. Don't know what it means."

"Interesting," Bud replied. "But Cal, one more question—no, two more. Have you heard anything about some kind of Black Beast up there? And you ever hear of something called the Slickrock Cafe?"

Cal looked surprised. "Didn't you just get into town? I'm surprised you know about that. There's been a rumor going around for a couple of weeks now that there's a black something running around up there, but nobody with any credibility's seen it, so I think it's just a rumor. As for the Slickrock Cafe, I dunno, but I kind of recall something about the old-time cowboys having get-togethers somewhere up there. That's as close as I know to what it could be. Maybe old Jack Pilling could help you out on that one."

"One more question," Bud said. "You ever heard of the Malachites?"

"Yeah, ain't that some tribe in the Old Testament?" Cal answered.

Bud turned to Krider, laughing. "See, I'm not the only one."

"What'd I say?" Cal asked, mystified.

"Naw, nothing," Bud replied. "Thanks, Cal. I'm heading back up to Green River tonight. I noticed you're on call. You contact me if anything important comes up. I'll be moving down here as soon as I can find a place."

"Roger," Cal said, then nodded goodbye to Krider and walked to the door. He then turned around, looking once more at Bud.

"Say, Sheriff, I hear things have got pretty liberal up there in Green River since you quit the sheriff's office, that right?" He pulled on his earlobe and grinned at Bud.

Bud answered, "Yeah, it's become a hotbed of anarchy, Cal. That new sheriff's made it so everyone's now required to get their ear pierced. Kind of like when Mayor Stocks wanted to make everyone here carry a gun."

Cal laughed. "You know I'm just kidding around, Bud. Welcome back."

Cal was still chuckling as he walked out.

Bud grimaced and turned to Krider. "Dammit. I knew I was in for a ribbing over this damn earring. At least the mayor didn't say anything."

Krider smiled. "That's cause he's probably thinking about getting one himself. You're going to start a new fashion runaway, Bud. I may get it done, too."

Bud shook his head. "If you were married to Wilma Jean, you would. Let's go on up to Slickrock. But first we need to do one more thing."

"What's that?" asked Krider.

"Get you your requisitioned firearm."

Krider's smile was gone. "Bud, you do know I've never fired a gun in my life?"

"Well, Prof, let's hope it stays that way," Bud replied.

CHAPTER 8

Bud's FJ toiled once again up the steep switchbacks to
Slickrock Flats, Krider reiterating everything Bud had
thought last time he was here.

"Man, if only I had a camera," Krider was saying. "This
is a photographer's paradise, Bud. This where you grew
up?"

"Pretty much," Bud answered, "though my family lived
in town. I spent half my childhood running around in these
wildlands."

He grinned again, fiddling with his earlobe while driving with one hand. He was obviously thinking about something.

Krider looked down at the steep drop below them. "You
mind using both hands?" he asked.

"I would, but I probably shouldn't try to drive with my
knees, Prof," Bud grinned. "Don't worry, I've been up this
so many times I could drive it in my sleep."

"Let me know before you decide to try," Krider laughed.

They soon topped out, and Bud pointed to the distant
Arrowhead, the place where he'd seen the Black Beast.
They stopped for a bit and got out, stretching their legs,
and were soon heading back up the road towards the Salt
Mountains.

"Maybe the Black Beast is your bête noire," Krider said.

"I don't know anyone named Bette," Bud replied.

"No, your anathema, Bud."

"I'm a what?" Bud asked.

Krider ignored Bud's bad puns. "Did you know that they call Bigfoot the Bête Noire in France?"

"No, I didn't know that, Prof. Also didn't know they had Bigfoot in France. But I don't think this was a Bigfoot. It was too low to the ground, too slinky. Besides, I don't believe in Bigfoot."

Krider looked at him knowingly. "After all that happened on the Swell?" He referred to Bud's last case.

"Nope," Bud paused, then added, "Well, maybe nope."

The road now began to narrow. Bud could see where it became one lane as it went between two huge fins.

"Jack's Crack," he pointed out. "Named after Jack Pilling, the rancher who leases the grazing rights up here. It was called the Lemon Squeeze before that."

Krider was amused. "Jack's Crack," he repeated. "Those old cowboys were a cheeky bunch. How in hellsbells could you run cattle up here? There's nothing to eat."

"It wasn't always like this. When I was a kid, there were deer here and grass up to your ankles everywhere. It's been overgrazed, which doesn't take much in this dry country. But it used to be wetter, too. The old cowboys talk about grass up to their stirrups."

The light dimmed as they entered the slot canyon between the fins, and it suddenly felt cooler.

"What do you do if you meet someone in here?" Krider asked.

"Just like everywhere else, the one going uphill has the right of way. The one going downhill has to back up. It's a matter of safety. It's safer backing uphill than down cause your engine will hold you back if your brakes fail."

They were soon through, and now Bud saw the big arrowhead-shaped rock on his left. He turned and parked under it. A faint trail led down from the road into the heart of the slickrock fins, the occasional juniper flanking it, with a pinion here and there where a small wash or basin would catch water, since pinions need more water than junipers.

They got out, and Bud handed Krider a shoulder holster, then showed him how to put it on. He then handed him a gun.

"I'm going to give you a real quick lesson in how to handle this thing, Prof. This is a Glock .40 caliber semi-automatic handgun. Here's how you hold it...here's the safety...here's how you put in the ammo. It holds 14 rounds in a clip with one already in the chamber. You have an extra clip in your shoulder holster. This thing will recoil a bit, so be prepared for that. It's best to not let anyone know you have it unless you intend to use it or you truly believe it will act as a deterrent. I prefer my Ruger, but this Glock is standard issue for Radium deputies. I'm giving it to you now just as a precaution, but it would be best we practice a bit somewhere before you actually have to use it—I hope we get to, anyway—practice, that is."

"Don't I need a license to carry concealed?" Krider asked, looking a bit intimidated.

"Not as a deputy," Bud answered.

"Wow, this could get serious, huh, Bud?"

"Prof, you know better than I do that someone that would murder once would do it twice. You write about it all the time. I'd sure hate to get you into something you regret, so if at anytime you change your mind, you can resign. I sure didn't anticipate being sheriff when I asked you to join me. I thought maybe we'd just be undercover on our own. Not as dangerous, maybe. I'm just hoping you don't decide to resign when I need you to cover me." Bud smiled.

"Well, Bud, it's all new to me, even though I write about it, there's something different about actually being out here. But I don't want to quit now, I'm actually really intrigued by all this. Since I'm only part-time, am I insured by the sheriff's office?" He half-joked.

"Actually, you are, Prof. But I sure don't want either of us to have to collect."

"Or our wives," Krider said solemnly.

• • •

The pair was now slowly walking down the old stock trail, looking for tracks or any hints that might help them solve what happened to Jimmy and Hum. The soft deep sand made the going difficult. All around them were long expanses of slickrock where the going would be easier, but they stuck to the trail, looking for clues.

It didn't take long to get to the small ledge where Hum had been found. They stopped and walked all around, but found nothing. The sand had been smoothed by the wind, and there were only a few fresh lizard tracks.

"Looks pretty clueless," Bud remarked. "I can't picture Hum tripping here and falling. He's too agile. He had to have been hit."

"You'd have to be looking elsewhere to fall over this," Krider conceded. They continued on down the trail, Bud stopping to check out where a coyote had recently crossed, leaving its prints before jumping onto a nearby rock and continuing.

Just then, Krider seemed to spot something. "Hey Bud, come over here."

He stood above a patch of cryptobiotic soil that had been crushed by something heavy. "What do you suppose did this?" he asked.

"Probably the same thing that did this," Bud replied, pointing to a large track nearby.

"That's huge!" said Krider. "What is it?"

"Looks like a cougar, but I've never seen one that big. It would dwarf two regular-sized cougars. Dang, I need a camera, Prof." He placed his hand in the print for scale. It easily spanned his.

"Could this be our Black Beast, Bud?" Krider asked.

Bud felt a bit of a chill. He could still see the dark creature of the other evening running towards him like a lightning bolt. He fiddled with the Ruger in its holster for a second, just to be sure it was still there, though he didn't know where else it would be.

"Let's see where it goes."

"Sure," Krider replied, his hand on the Glock under his jacket flap. It made him feel more secure, though he didn't even know how to use it. If all else failed, he could use it for head-whacking, he figured.

They tracked it for fifty feet or so to where it jumped onto the slickrock and disappeared.

"Could be right over there, watching us right now," Bud pointed to a small black alcove in a nearby fin. "OK, let's see if we can find the tree they found Jimmy under."

"Wait, Bud, look at this," Krider said.

Not far from the last track, on a sandstone boulder the size of a car, a design had been carved into the rock. Bud and Krider both examined it.

"It's some kind of picture," Krider said, "or symbol." He walked closer to it.

"It's a cougar head," Bud replied. "But it looks weird. Why do I get the feeling I've seen this before?"

"Because you probably have. It's a cougar, all right, but it's stylized, like the ancient Incas. You read anything about the Incas, and you'll see this cougar. It looks exactly like the one I saw a few months ago in the Museo de Anthropoligia in Mexico City. In fact, all Incan cougars, or what they call pumas further south, look like this. The puma was one of their major symbols, it meant good luck to see one."

Bud examined it closer. "I can do without good luck, then. But this wasn't done by no Incan, Prof," he said. "Look at the chisel lines. This was done recently. Like really recently. There's no weathering of any kind. Fresh."

Krider studied the carving. "Sure looks like it, doesn't it? I wonder if this is related to Jimmy's death."

"Well, at least we're not clueless anymore," Bud said. "I sure need a camera."

They went back to the trail, then on down a bit to where a large pinion tree stood, a deep three-foot gash in its trunk where a porcupine had made lunch of its bark. It was an old tree, nearly 20 feet tall, big for a pinion in this dry-bone desert, thought Bud. For some reason the tree had an air of familiarity to it, but Bud couldn't quite place it.

They carefully looked around under it, but found nothing.

"Nothing much here," remarked Bud, turning to Krider, but the prof was no longer there to answer—he had disappeared.

Bud turned all around, looking. How could Krider just flat out disappear like that? He started calling out, "Hey, Prof! Prof!"

"No need to yell," Krider replied. "Up here."

Bud craned his neck to see Krider high in the pinion tree.

"What the hell are you doing up there?"

Krider shimmied back down the tree, bringing a barrage of small branches and the sweet smell of pine with him. He brushed off his tweed jacket, then held something up to Bud.

"This," he said, simply, holding up a chunk of rich-green rock the size of a large walnut.

"How in heck did you spot that? It was up in the tree?" Bud asked.

"The sun caught it just right," Krider answered. "It's malachite, Bud, malachite. Gem quality."

Just then, a distant scream made their blood chill.

Bud knew that scream, and it wasn't that far away.

"Get the hell out, now!" he said. "It must have heard me yelling."

With that, they both began running back up the trail, the deep sand slowing them down until their legs and lungs burned like the fire on the redrock above Radium at sunset.

CHAPTER 9

Bud and Professor Krider tumbled into the FJ, locking the doors behind them, then sat and puffed for awhile, watching the back trail out the front window.

Finally, after catching his breath, Bud said, "Wow! I haven't run like that since the night Wilma Jean's dad found out I proposed to her."

A hint of amusement crossed Krider's face, then he said, "Dang, Bud, how can you joke around at a time like this? That creature could come up on us any second. Let's get out of here. Where do you think it is?"

Bud replied, "I think it's still right where it was when we first heard it."

"How so?" Krider asked.

"Well, Prof, I know I ran like a scared rabbit, but as I was running, a lot of blood was diverted from my brain into my lungs, making my brain stop interfering with my gut for a bit and giving me a new perspective on things. That scream was exactly like the first one I heard. To put it succinctly, exactly."

"You mean, you think it was faked?"

"I can't be sure, but my gut says it was. It had a bit of a mechanical sound to it."

Krider had a puzzled look on his face. "I think you're right, but I've never heard a cougar scream before to compare. But it was a bit loud for the distance it seemed to be covering. But it was good enough that we both ran."

"True enough," Bud replied. "But possibly next time we'll know better."

"You think someone's trying to scare people off?"

"Maybe. There seems to be a lot of action near that Porky Tree lately—Jimmy was killed there and Hum was whacked over the head not far away. Seems to be a hot spot for some reason."

"Someone's trying to hide something? Like the Malachites, whatever they are?"

"Seems like a sound theory to me, Prof."

"Why would there be a chunk of malachite up in the tree?"

"I think that chunk shows that the Malachites, whatever they are, must be nearby."

"But a rock up in a tree?"

"Ravens. I studied ravens a bunch when I was a kid up here. I even had a couple that would follow me around cause I always fed them. I learned a lot by watching them. Ravens will carry food a ways and cache it, sometimes quite a ways if they think another bird's watching. They also like to pick up baubles and colorful things, but, unlike food, they lose interest and won't carry them far, they just drop them in midair."

Krider whistled. "I'll be darned. A raven picked up a piece of malachite nearby and lost interest right over that tree."

"That would be my guess," Bud replied. "But it's getting late. And if you don't mind, I'd like to stop by the Uranium

Diner and grab a cup of coffee before we head home. It's bound to be busy this time of day, and I'd like to just soak up the ambience."

"Ambience in a diner?" Krider asked.

"Maybe 'buzz' is a better word," Bud replied, starting the FJ and backing onto the Slickrock Flats Road.

• • •

Bud opened the door to the diner and was hit by a cloud of steam and noise. The place was packed, but he and Krider managed to find a booth in the back, which was where Bud always liked to sit anyway, where he could study people. They pulled menus from a metal holder on the table.

"Might as well have dinner," Bud said, not sure if Wilma Jean was expecting him for dinner or not. She would be at the bowling alley by the time he got home.

"Fine by me," Krider replied. "What's good?"

"Boy, I dunno. Haven't eaten here for a long time. Their green-chile burgers used to be really good. That's what I think I'll get."

"Sounds like a recipe for nightmares," Krider said. "I think I'll get the chicken-fried snake, I mean steak."

Bud wasn't sure—maybe he'd have what the prof was getting after all. He casually glanced around to see if there were anyone here he recognized. He spotted a couple of familiar faces, but not anyone he knew well, just the cashier at the grocery store and a few folks like that.

Then he noticed someone he did know—and knew well—in the booth right across from theirs. He carefully nodded to Krider. "Sonny Ottin right there," he said quietly. "Jimmy's son."

Krider casually turned to look. Sonny had hair so blonde it was almost white, what you could see of it, as he was wearing a beat-up straw cowboy hat. He was tanned and fit looking and appeared to be about Bud's age.

For some reason, Bud hoped Sunny wouldn't notice him. He pulled his cowboy hat down around his temples and began fiddling with his ear-post.

"Hoping he won't see you?" Krider asked quietly.

"Yeah, but I don't know why. We go way back. Kind of grew up together."

Just then the waitress came to take their orders.

● ● ●

After they ate, they ordered coffee and sat and watched everyone in the diner. Sonny had also finished his dinner and was now studying what looked to be an appointment book. He seemed to be somewhat lost in another world, barely noticing the one around him, Bud thought.

Just then, the door opened and a tall thin man entered. Bud recognized this man—it was Deputy Rohr. He was out of uniform, dressed like someone from the city with his shiny black shoes and knee-length wool jacket. Bud held a menu up to his face and looked over its edge.

Rohr looked around a bit, then, noticing Sonny, came directly back and sat down across from him. Bud strained to hear what was said, but the diner was noisy and he could only make out a few words. Sonny wrote something down in his little book, then Rohr handed him a wad of bills and got up and left. Sonny silently counted the money and put it into his jacket pocket, looked around, then retreated back into his own world. He obviously hadn't noticed Bud.

No sooner had he done this then another man entered the diner and headed his way. Bud recognized this man—it was rancher Jack Pilling of Jack's Crack fame. Bud intended to go see Jack tomorrow when he and Krider came back down from Green River. Bud pulled his hat down further and put his hand on his chin.

Jack had a loud booming voice, and Bud had no trouble at all hearing him. In fact, Jack's nickname around town was "Whispering Jack."

"Howdy, Sonny. How's life treating you?" Jack sat down.

Bud couldn't hear Sonny's reply.

"I'm sure glad I spotted you," Jack said. "Here's the money I owe you." Bud saw him hand Sonny a wad of cash, just like Hans.

Sonny mumbled something, then Jack replied, "No, I don't need any now, I'm fine, but thanks, anyway. We sure miss your dad, Son. Gotta go, if I'm late for dinner my wife's gonna crack me over the head."

Bud, still surreptitiously looking out from under his hat, noted that Sonny winced at Jack's words.

Jack stood and was soon gone, his voice booming out greetings to others until he walked out the diner.

Bud looked knowingly at Krider, then said quietly, "What the hell?"

"Maybe drugs or maybe dino bone, eh?" Krider answered.

"Why would Rohr and Jack want either?"

"No idea," Krider replied, taking a long sip of coffee. "But never underestimate the needs and wants of your fellow man."

"Agreed," Bud answered, "Nor underestimate that their motives are probably different from yours."

He stood, pushed his hat back, and went over to the booth where Sonny sat.

"Evening, Sonny. How's everything?" Bud asked.

Sonny looked up. Looks of recognition and shock came over his face at the same time.

"I'll be go to. Bud Shumway."

Sonny stood, offering Bud his hand, and they shook warmly.

"Have a seat, Bud. What brings you down this way?"

"I heard about your dad, Sonny," Bud replied, evading the answer. "I'm sure sorry. He was one of my heroes."

"Mine, too," Sonny answered glumly. "When I wasn't ready to kill him." He twitched, realizing what he'd just said. "Not that I would have," he added.

"Do you know anything about what happened?"

"Not much. Only that he was murdered. Nobody's saying how until the investigation is closed."

"Was he shot?" Bud asked.

"Dunno," Sonny answered, his eyes suddenly clouded. "Just don't know, nobody's saying."

"Well, I'm sorry to ask," Bud said. "I feel like I lost a part of my family, I can tell you that, Sonny, and I can also tell you I'm gonna find who did it."

Sonny looked up, surprised. "You are?"

"I am. It's my new personal goal. Your dad meant a lot to me." He stood. "Well, gotta run, but I'll be seeing you around. You out at the rock shop?"

"Yeah, I'm taking it over, now that Dad's gone. I wasn't making any money cowboying anyway—if I'm gonna be broke, might as well be able to sleep in my own bed."

Bud noted that Sunny was now studying his ear-post. Sonny then shrugged his shoulders, saying nothing.

"You were cowboying? I didn't know that."

"Yup. Old Man Pilling."

"Jack? He would be a harsh taskmaster, if I know him."

"He was. But he's fair. Paid better than my dad."

"Well, you take care, and I'll stop by soon."

"You do that, Bud, you're always welcome."

Sonny stood, then added, "Bud, you be careful. There's weird stuff going on, and I'd hate to see you get hurt. You should leave the investigation up to the sheriff."

With that, Sonny was out the door.

Krider and Bud were soon behind, Bud feeling around in his jacket pocket for some Tums, already regretting his dinner choice.

CHAPTER 10

Bud pulled into his drive in Green River, having dropped
Krider off, glad to be home. It was dark, and Wilma Jean
had left the porch light on, which meant she probably
wasn't too mad at him for showing up so late. She was
gone anyway, down at the bowling alley.

The dogs greeted him at the door as if they thought
they had been abandoned forever, Hoppie barking, and
Pierre chomping onto his pant leg and dragging along as
Bud walked. After having the little dog for a few months,
Bud had come to the conclusion that this was just how his
life was going to be from now on, having his own personal
dachshund welcoming committee.

As he walked into the kitchen, he saw a package on the
kitchen table. It had a little note attached that read, "Hon,
for you, hope you like it. XXOO"

Bud took off his jacket, then put his gun into the gun
safe. He then took the package with him into the living
room, where he sat down in his big comfy chair, Pierre still
dragging along behind him, attached to his pant leg and
growling.

Wilma Jean had obviously been shopping. That meant
she'd gone up to Price, a good hour away, or over to Grand

Junction, a couple of hours, but with more places to buy things. He guessed Price, since he knew she had things to do at the cafe and bowling alley.

He leaned back, causing the chair's footrest to pop out, then tried to kick his feet up, forgetting all about Pierre, who went for a little flight in the process, landing on the footrest along with Bud's feet.

"Oh jeezlouise, Pierre," Bud said with concern. He pictured the little weener dog in a flight scarf and helmet like Snoopy's. "You OK? You should let go when your feet start to leave the ground."

Pierre now let go, tumbling to the carpet.

Bud patted Pierre's head, then set to opening the package. It wasn't very big, nor was it heavy. He had no idea what it could be until he found a sticker on it that read "Price's Right Cameras and Electronics," and then, when he got through the first layer of plastic, the word "Canon."

Inside was a pretty powder-pink Canon camera, all automatic, the kind that fit in your pocket. Bud sat for a bit and looked at it, not sure whether to feel appreciative or disappointed. It was a camera, all right, the exact same kind he'd carried as Sheriff of Emery County, yet not quite what he had in mind as a budding professional photographer. But yet, it was a camera, and better than what he'd had, which was nothing. He wasn't so sure about the color, though.

He fiddled with it, putting the memory card in and taking a few photos of the dogs. It seemed to work well, and he knew it would take good photos, but everything was automatic, and you couldn't change lenses, you were stuck with what you got.

Oh well, he sighed. It was awfully sweet of Wilma Jean to think of him like that. He'd have to get her some flowers soon.

Just then, his phone rang.

"Yell-ow," he answered.

"Bud, it's Cal, down here in Radium. You said to call if anything important came up. Well, it has."

Cal had caught Bud by surprise. "It has?"

"It sure has," Cal answered. "Some young guy was out hiking up at Slickrock and said he was chased. He described it as a huge black cougar, so maybe the rumor's not such a rumor after all. He managed to roll under a small ledge where it couldn't get to him and dialed 911. We went out there and found him and got him out. Just thought you'd like to know."

"Thanks, Cal. Do you have his phone number?" Bud paused, writing down the number, then continued. "Listen, I don't want anyone up there tonight. Can you go block the road, then cruise and make sure there's nobody camping? Anyone else on duty right now?"

"Hans."

"OK, Cal. Take him with you. I was up there earlier and didn't see any campers, but if there are, run them off."

"You seem to be thinking it's pretty dangerous, huh, Bud? Most cougars won't bother you. The kid had been jogging, and that triggers an attack instinct in them. I doubt if it's anything that merits shutting the place down. Maybe we should go hunting tomorrow."

"Cal, what I didn't mention earlier was that I've seen the damn thing myself. Believe me, it's not a normal cougar. There's something going on, and I don't want anyone else hurt. And no hunting—not yet, anyway."

"Roger, Bud, will get right on it."

"OK, Cal, and be careful."

• • •

Bud read the paper for a bit, then decided to call the hospital and see how Hum was doing. He'd wanted to stop by there earlier, but he knew they wouldn't let him into the room.

"Radium Memorial. How may I direct your call?"

So, they did have a receptionist after all, he mused. "Room 121, please."

"Hello." It was Peggy Sue.

"Hi, Peg. Bud here. How's everything going?"

"Oh Bud, hey Bud, good to hear from you. Helen told me about how they ran you out. I can't believe they would do that, and I told them so. But between her and me, we're coping. There's no change in Hum, he's still off somewhere else."

"Peg, I haven't had a chance to tell you, but he woke up when I was there. I was going to call you later, but you needed your sleep, then I got so dang busy I forgot. He actually even talked to me a bit. And he can hear what's going on around him down there, so talk to him. You be sure and tell his doctor, OK?"

"OK," she said. "That's fantastic."

Bud noted she seemed to be in better spirits.

"Oh, Bud," she continued, "Earl called me. You and Wilma Jean stay in our basement until things get settled a bit. I mean, until Hum wakes up and you can quit or until he..." She faded out.

"That would be great, Peg. I may end up just going back and forth for a bit, but if things get too crazy and they need me down there, we'll need a place to stay. Much appreciated."

"I wouldn't mind having you guys around, and Earl said they'd pay me a bit of rent, which would help. Wilma Jean and I need to catch up. It has a guest bedroom and bath, and a big den, and you can use the kitchen upstairs."

"You do know we have dogs?"

"I know. They can play with Grid."

Bud laughed. That name always got him, Grid Bias. Hum was a HAM radio operator and he'd named their little brown mutt after something to do with a radio part.

"OK," he continued. "You hang in there, and be sure to call if anything changes. See if you can work on getting me back in there to talk to Hum again."

"I will," Peggy Sue replied. "I'll ask the doctor next time I see him."

• • •

Bud got up and went into the kitchen, made some microwave popcorn, then sat back down just in time for his phone to ring again. He was beginning to remember how it had been when he was sheriff here—he never had any time to himself, and he was always where the buck stopped. The stress had finally got to him, and he'd quit. He knew he could never be sheriff again anywhere, and was once again grateful for his farm job.

"Yell-ow," he mumbled through a mouthful of popcorn.

It was Cal again.

"Sheriff, me and Hans are up here at Slickrock, and there's a motorcycle gang setting up camp, and they won't leave. We're seriously outnumbered. Please advise."

Bud noted how different it was talking to Cal than to Howie. Cal got right to the point.

"A motorcycle gang? Is it the Minot Marauders? How many—about a dozen?"

"How'd you know that?" Cal asked. "And they're not co-operating. I told them to clear out, and they say they don't have anywhere else to go."

"Did you tell them why?"

"Yup. They said they're not worried."

"OK. Tell them they can stay, but the road's shut down and they're not coming out until we open it back up tomorrow. Write up a statement that they're staying at their own risk, and get every single one of them to sign it."

"10-4."

With that, Bud turned off his cell phone and turned on the TV. Tonight was his favorite show, and Radium would just have to get by without him.

He flipped through the channels, then kicked back. Pierre sighed and snuggled next to him while Hoppie lay at his feet, everyone watching Scooby Doo.

CHAPTER 11

Bud sat in his office, wearing the uniform of Radium County Sheriff, khaki shirt and pants, not much different than what he usually wore. He used to wear only blue jeans, but he found the khaki was more comfortable for sitting on a tractor most of the day, plus a bit cooler. His only complaint was that the lighter color showed when he managed to spill coffee on himself.

Professor Krider sat across from him, wearing the same outfit. Bud noted that Krider seemed to have an almost continual look of bemusement about him these days. He figured he must be enjoying his new job as deputy.

Bud pulled a number from his pocket and dialed it. A young man's voice answered.

"This is Sheriff Bud Shumway," Bud said, "Is Pete Tallman there?"

"That's me," the voice said.

"Pete, could you tell me what happened last night up at Slickrock when you were hiking?"

"Oh man, Sheriff, that was really something. I was out hiking, then I noticed it was getting late, so I turned around and started jogging back up the trail. I came on out of the canyon and was on top when I heard the most horrible scream. It gives me the creeps right now to talk about it. I turned around in that direction, and I saw this black cougar coming up the trail behind me. I started running, but I could tell there was no way I could outrun it, so I saw a ledge and managed to crawl up under it."

"Sounds pretty frightening," Bud commiserated. "Where exactly were you?"

"I had hiked down that old stock trail out by the Arrowhead, clear down into Granstaff Canyon. I sat there by the stream for a bit, then noticed the sun was going down, so that's when I came back."

"Where did you see this cougar or whatever it was?"

"It was about where that big pinion tree is, the one with the big porcupine scar on its trunk. I was ahead of that, only maybe a couple of tenths of a mile on up the trail, not that far from my car when I saw it. Man, that thing was fast, and I mean fast. What do you think it is?"

"We're not sure yet, Pete, but we've closed the area down, at least for a bit until we can check it out. Were you hurt in any way?"

"No, Sir, just my pride while I was under that ledge hiding like a kangaroo rat, hoping there weren't any snakes under there with me. But I'm not going back out there until you guys get that thing. Too dangerous."

"Well, that's probably a good idea," Bud said. "One more thing—did this black thing try to get to you under the ledge? What exactly happened then?"

"No, it seemed to just disappear. It never even came near me, thank God."

"That's good, Pete. Thanks for the information. You have a good day."

Bud pushed his chair back and began fiddling with his ear-post. He then stood up and grabbed his jacket.

"Prof, let's get on up there and see what's going on. Cal left that motorcycle gang up there with the road closed down. Earl's on duty today, it's his last day, and he said he hasn't had a chance to get up there and check on things. Let's go see if anyone's still alive."

• • •

Bud topped out on the Dump Road, then started up the next switchback to Slickrock Flats, where a sign informed him the road was closed ahead. Once on top, he could see where Cal had put up a temporary roadblock.

Sitting on the far side were two men in black leathers on motorcycles, and on this side was a pickup with a stock rack with horseshoes welded onto it in a pattern proclaiming the 4 Bar Ranch, though it looked more like the 4 Bent Horseshoes Ranch to Bud.

He pulled up next to the pickup. A tall older wiry man dressed in denim jeans and jacket and faded felt cowboy hat was standing at the roadblock, face red and drawn like he was about to have a heart attack.

It was Jack Pilling. He appeared to be arguing with the motorcycle riders, which probably wasn't a very good idea, Bud surmised.

Bud then changed his mind and decided it wasn't a good idea on the motorcyclists' part to argue, once he saw that Jack was carrying a rifle.

Jack was known for his hot temper, and he'd even shot at Bud's uncle once years ago when he thought he was poaching deer. It turned out that Jack had a pet deer he'd raised from a fawn and didn't recognize Bud's uncle, a wildlife officer who had stopped by the highway above Jack's ranch to look for poachers.

They managed to get through the confusion without anyone getting shot, but Jack was always grateful to Bud's uncle for not throwing him in jail, and that gratitude seemed to have filtered down to Bud, who Jack seemed to like. The incident was the last straw for Bud's uncle, who quit the wildlife department, setting a record for shortest length of employment there.

"Howdy, Jack," Bud stepped from his FJ, Krider by his side.

"Nice to see you, Bud," Jack replied. "These thugs here are trying to break down this barricade the sheriff put up, and I'm saying that's a no go, even though it's keeping me from going home myself. But the law's the law. These fellas need to go get jobs and become contributing members of society like the rest of us."

The motorcycle riders didn't look amused and revved their engines for a moment, making a statement, drowning out everything else. They didn't look like the types one would want to have mad at them, but Jack didn't seem to notice.

"Well, Jack, we're here to take that roadblock down, so thanks for manning the fort for us," Bud replied.

Jack bristled a bit. "No offense, Bud, but you can't just take it down neither, that's the sheriff's job."

Bud grinned and pointed to his badge, then Krider's. It seemed to take Jack a minute to comprehend what he was looking at, then he snorted, "You're the sheriff? Since when?"

Bud was already taking down the barricade. "Since day before yesterday, Jack," he grunted as he and Krider carried it off the road. "I'm Interim Sheriff until Hum gets back."

The bikers revved their bikes again, then took off with a roar that echoed off the cliffs. Jack shook his fist at them and yelled, "You devil's minions better mend your ways!" They ignored him and were soon gone, echoing on down the hill into Radium.

"Jack, those guys could eat your lunch in one bite, and they sure wouldn't pick up the tab," Bud cautioned. "Better exercise a little restraint around them."

"Hell, I ain't scared one bit," Jack said. "I betcha they're all bankers and lawyers out on a lark, trying to be tough. Minot, North Dakota, my ass. I been there once. Damn scary place," he mocked.

"Never know," Bud replied. "But hey, we're going up to your place here in a bit, if that's OK."

"What for?" Jack asked suspiciously.

"I just want to ask you a few things—there's lots going on in your backyard, you know."

"Ain't nothing I know about," Jack said defensively. "But hell, come on up. But don't expect Melba to be too happy after me spending the night out playing poker. Maybe I'll just tell her I couldn't get home because of the roadblock, it did detain me for a bit. Say, why did you have the road blocked, anyway?"

"We'll tell you when we come up, Jack. That's part of why we want to talk to you. See you later."

• • •

Driving on up the Slickrock Road, Bud pulled over to let Jack go around, as he was now tailgating. Jack honked and spun out on the gravel as he passed, fishtailing a bit.

Krider commented, "Man, what a character. They broke the mold after they made him."

"I sure hope so," Bud replied.

He pulled over into the campground, where the Minot Marauders were now in various stages of lounging around, a few playing horseshoes and the rest sitting in camp chairs around a campfire, talking and drinking what looked to be beer, even though it wasn't even yet noon.

"Let's stop and have a visit with the devil's minions, Prof."

He and Krider got out just as Bud's phone rang.

"Yell-ow," Bud answered, leaning against his FJ.

Krider walked on over to the group, not waiting for Bud.

"Sheriff, it's Howie. Hope I'm not catching you at a bad time, but I need to talk to you."

"Go ahead, Howie, but I can't talk long. The devil's minions are waiting for me."

"The what?"

"Never mind. What's up?"

"Well, Bud, I just heard a rumor that Radium's the site for a big motorcycle gang get-together. I mean a big one. It seems like the Minot Marauders are organizing it, and Bud, they have a real bad reputation."

"You've heard of the Minot Marauders?"

"They're bad ones, Bud."

"Where did you hear this, Howie?"

"Maureen said she heard someone down at the Melon Rind talking about it. She's working for Wilma Jean there now, though I'm sure you already know that."

Bud didn't know that. He realized he hadn't talked to Wilma Jean except briefly by phone for going on some time now.

"Was it just talk, Howie, or was it someone reliable?"

"I dunno, Bud. You be careful down there. I checked it out on the internet, and Minot used to be a tough railroad town, and it was once called Little Chicago. It's where Capone brought liquor in from Canada during Prohibition."

"Howie, that was in the 1920s, a long time ago."

"I know, but these kinds of towns never get over their bad reputations, Sheriff. They usually end up deciding to just go with it and stay bad. Be careful. Over." He hung up.

Howie couldn't have timed that one better if he'd tried, Bud thought. He could see Krider over by the fire, talking to the bikers, and he wondered if the prof were in any danger.

No more had the thought gone through his mind than he saw Krider jump, then take off running as fast as he could, coming back towards the FJ. The gang likewise jumped up, chairs scattering, chasing close behind.

Bud jumped behind the vehicle for protection and drew his Ruger, thinking about how fast things change, as he saw several gang members pull guns from beneath their black leather jackets.

CHAPTER 12

Krider ran around behind the FJ where Bud was, his eyes big and face white.

"I'm scared to death of snakes," he said in a shaky voice.

The Minot Marauders were now next to Bud's FJ, laughing and milling around excitedly.

"Fellas, don't shoot it," Bud said, coming out from behind the FJ. "I'll take care of it."

"Are you gonna shoot it?" A big bald burley guy with tattoos all over asked, nodding towards Bud's Ruger.

Bud put it back in its holster. "No, I was just checking my gun out," he said, then asked, "What exactly was it, Prof?"

"A snake. I don't know what kind, I didn't stick around long enough to ask."

"It was a big fat rattler," someone said. "They'd just as soon kill you as go fishin'."

Bud holstered his gun, then slowly made his way over to where chairs and beer cans and still-burning cigars lay on the ground in various states of chaos. He carefully looked around, but didn't see a snake. He then walked around the perimeter of the camp and, sure enough, he found a big bullsnake hiding under a rabbitbrush, its tail sticking out. Bud thought it looked terrified, if snakes can be terrified.

"What it is? A rattler?" Most of the Minot Marauders were behind Bud, hanging back, but curious.

"No, it's a bullsnake," Bud replied.

"Is it dangerous? Will it bite?" someone asked.

"It won't hurt you. They mostly eat rodents."

"It's a rattler. It curled up and looked like it was gonna strike, like a rattlesnake does," a small wiry guy with a nose ring said.

Bud replied, "Bullsnakes are smart. They've learned how to fake it and will act like a rattler when cornered. They've been known to bite under duress, but they're not poisonous."

He gently prodded the snake with a stick, trying to get it to come out. He wanted to get it far away from the camp for its own protection. He'd grown up out in this country and had a lot of respect for its other citizens. The snake soon began slowly slithering across the sand, then stopped.

The biker gang stood back, cautious but curious, watching. Bud got behind the snake and deftly grabbed it behind its head, rendering it helpless. The snake dangled down a good three feet, and the gang again scattered.

"Guys, I'm gonna relocate this snake, and if it comes back, nobody better hurt it. It's harmless, and we like these guys, they keep the rodents down and will even run rattlers out if they come into their territory." With that, he carried the snake a good ways off and released it.

When he came back, he felt a change. The gang seemed to be a bit in awe of his snake-handling abilities. City boys, Bud thought to himself, wondering how big Minot was.

Bud began asking questions, curious if anyone had heard or seen anything strange during the night. No one had. He carefully explained that there was a black cougar out here and they should be careful, but they assured him they weren't doing any hiking, but were just hanging around camp.

Just then he heard the sound of motorcycles coming, and the pair that had been at the roadblock drove up. The lead biker parked his bike and got off, half-swaggering over to Bud and Krider while taking off his black leather gloves. He had long hair tied in a ponytail and wore a red bandanna tied around his head. The second was very muscular and looked like he worked out all day, wore a green bandanna, and had a tattoo on his forearm that read "Snoopy." Bud hid his smile, as neither looked like anyone Bud would want to tangle with.

"What's going on here, Sheriff?" asked the first, who appeared from his demeanor to be the gang leader. Bud noted that he seemed used to being in charge and wasn't overly friendly. Bud also noted that he had both of his ears pierced and wore ear-posts just like Bud's.

Before Bud could answer, a couple of bikers did it for him, explaining about the snake and the Black Beast. The leader seemed to soften a bit, and Bud decided it would be a good time to ask what was going on.

"I heard a rumor you guys were planning a big party here in Radium, one involving some other biker gangs, is that true?"

The leader nudged his cohort and broke into a grin. "Where'd you hear that?"

"From another sheriff on up the way," Bud replied. "I hope it's not true, but if it is, you fellas need to be aware that you're camping right smack in the middle of redneck country, and I might not be able to ensure the peace if you get out of hand. There's plenty of guys around here who might have some outdated notions about bikers, and they all exercise their constitutional rights to bear arms, just as I see you guys do."

Krider looked admiringly at Bud, wishing he had a notepad to write down what he'd just said. It would make a good line somewhere in a book, he thought, a diplomatic way of saying bad bikers aren't tolerated in these parts.

Now the fellow who appeared to be next in command spoke, "Sheriff, Barry here would never let us get out of hand like that, even if we wanted to. He's one tough hombre." He poked Barry in the ribs, grinning.

The leader, who Bud now took to be named Barry, answered, "Jeff's right, Sheriff. We're not trouble-makers, and whoever started that rumor is who you need to get after, not us."

Bud relaxed. There wouldn't be any trouble, at least not here and now. He replied, "Well, that's good, boys, you keep it quiet and Radium will welcome your business. There's lots to see and do around here, and if you treat the locals right, they'll do you the same in return. And we have a strict no-shooting rule here in the Slickrock Flats Recreation Area. Have a nice day."

He got into the FJ, Krider close behind, and drove away, leaving the bikers standing by the road, eating his dust and probably still worrying about snakes, Bud figured.

CHAPTER 13

"Bud, I think you made an impression on those fellows," Krider smiled as they wound up the road on their way to Jack Pilling's ranch, which set on the mesa above Slickrock Flats.

Bud didn't reply, twiddling with his ear-post. Krider could tell he was thinking about something.

They wound upwards, leaving the slickrock fins and coming into a juniper forest on a flat mesa. The Salt Mountains towered above them with their cloaks of snow, and below they could see far into the distant desert, clear over to the Bookcliffs above Green River.

Finally, Bud said, "Prof, did you notice that Barry had his ears pierced? What do you think of that guy?"

Krider replied, "Well, he's obviously the pack leader. And he struck me as being very intelligent. He's used to being in command, and I bet none of them are professional bikers. It's a weekend gang, Bud, and they have money."

"How do you know all that?"

"First of all, they all drive BMWs, which aren't cheap, with fancy custom panniers and all that. And they're all pretty much stock bikes. The Harley-Davidson bunch tends to customize their bikes, but when you own an expensive bike like a BMW, you don't so much, as you want it to keep its value. Not that Harleys are cheap, but they're not like BMWs."

"Good point, But how do you know they're weekenders?"

"Because they're all white as ghosts, Bud, except that Jeff fellow, and I'll bet he works outside at something physical. Real bikers don't typically work inside much, in fact, they usually don't have real jobs, and they're out on their bikes. They usually have dark tans on their faces and arms. None of these guys did, except Jeff."

"Good observation," Bud said. "You should write murder mysteries."

Krider laughed as they pulled up to a closed gate with a sign that read, "The 4 Bar Ranch."

• • •

The gate barely held together a barbed wire fence in various stages of disrepair. Jack's getting old, and he's letting things slip, Bud thought. Just a few years ago, Jack would never have let his fences get like this, he was proud of his place. Maybe he couldn't afford to hire help.

Wired to the fence were handmade signs warning people of all the bad things that would happen to them if they entered.

"Trespassers will be shot first and then arrested," read one. Another read, simply, "Beware." And, "Trespassers here are shot and skinned, but not necessarily in that order."

Bud was kind of amused, but kind of not. Jack seemed to be getting more and more crotchety as he got older, and

Bud was worried he would someday shoot some innocent hiker who had crossed the fence down the line, unaware he was trespassing.

Krider had managed to wrestle the wire gate open so Bud could drive on through, then closed it behind him.

"Man, that guy sure doesn't want anyone in here, does he? I hope he doesn't shoot us."

"Prof, I wonder if Jack would shoot someone in the back?" Bud asked.

"He seems like he could get trigger happy without too much forethought," Krider answered. "One of those guys the anti-gun people hold up when arguing their case, but I don't know about in the back. You think he had something to do with Jimmy Ottin's death?"

"I just don't know," Bud replied. "But Jack has the grazing rights to the area where Jimmy and Hum were both found, and he's got an explosive personality. I can't see him hitting Hum over the head, but I could see him shooting Jimmy if the circumstances were right. I hope I'm wrong about that."

"What kind of gun was it?"

"A Browning A-Bolt rifle. They're made right here in Utah."

Well, let's keep an eye out and see what he has, Bud," Krider said as they came up to an old ranch house surrounded by tall lilac bushes and big cottonwood trees.

Two big black dogs came out to greet them, both gray around the muzzles and wagging their tails. A dark green compact car sat in the driveway.

Bud knocked on the door, but no one answered. He then noticed there was neither hide nor hair of Jack's pickup—he must be further up on the mesa, Bud thought, as they hadn't passed him coming up. He knocked again, only louder.

Finally, an older woman answered the door. She looked tired, her gray hair pulled back in a ponytail—just like Barry's, Bud mused. She seemed irritated until she saw who it was, then opened the screen door and stepped out.

"I can't believe my eyes, it's Bud Shumway." She squeezed his shoulder affectionately. "And wearing a sheriff's badge. You our new sheriff now, Bud?" She suddenly seemed reserved, but motioned for them to come in.

"Thanks, Melba, it's good to see you, too. I'm the Interim Sheriff until Hum comes back."

"I didn't even know he was gone. Where'd he go?" she asked.

"He's gone into a world none of us know much about," Bud offered, not really wanting to discuss it. "Is Jack around?"

"Jack? He'd better not be," she answered with disgust, seeming to relax now that she knew why Bud was there. "I ran him off about an hour ago. He was out all night playing poker. He comes in, just like nothing's happened, like he went out for a cup of coffee, hoping I won't care, but I do. I'm sick and tired of it, having to be alone up here all night with who knows what while he sends us to the poorhouse. I'm going to move in with my sister up in Price. Her husband had a heart attack a couple of years ago and she's been after me ever since to leave Jack. I'm taking the dogs and leaving in one week."

"Does Jack know that?" Bud asked. "By the way, this is Deputy Krider."

"Nice meeting you, too bad we didn't meet when I was in a better mood. You're not seeing my best side here."

"I understand," Krider replied.

She answered Bud, "Jack knows. You boys want some coffee?"

"Sure," Bud replied, not wanting to turn down her hospitality and also hoping maybe Jack would come back in the meantime. "Where'd Jack go, Melba?"

"Oh, where he always goes. We've been playing this game for years, way too many years, I can tell you that. He leaves for awhile, waits for me to simmer down, then comes back. He's getting worse and worse, gambling what little we don't have. We can't even afford to hire anybody now that Sonny left, and this place is going to hell in a handbasket."

"But where does he go?" Bud asked again.

"He says he's going down to the Slickrock Cafe, Bud, but he actually goes into town. I have no idea where the Slickrock Cafe actually is, but I know it's not down in town. It's some place where the cowboys have been meeting for years, down in the slickrock, is all I know. It started out as a rendezvous place for the cattle drives, back when they had enough grass to run lots of cattle, and it evolved into a place where they just go to drink, would be my guess. You ever heard of the Arbuckle Cafe? It's like that."

Bud had no idea what the Arbuckle Cafe was, but Krider was now asking Melba if Jack had any rifles around.

"He has several, they're over in that gun case. I'll be right back with the coffee."

Bud and Krider went to the gun case, which was in the corner of the living room. It was unlocked. In it were two old rifles—a Winchester and a Remington, but no Browning.

Melba came back into the room, holding the handle of an old percolator coffee pot with a potholder. She then went back into the kitchen, bringing back a tray with cups, cream, sugar, and spoons on it, along with a plate of homemade chocolate-chip cookies. She poured them each a cup of steamy black coffee.

"Help yourself, boys," she said. "You know, I'm sorry to be in such a bad mood, and I don't normally tell everyone about my private life, but I've just had it with that man. And you know, he's getting harder and harder to deal with. I think he's getting senile or something."

"How so?" Krider asked.

"Well, he's always grouchy any more. He didn't used to be that way. And after years of my hounding him, he finally quit smoking, only to replace it with the most disgusting habit on earth—chew. But I shouldn't bad mouth my own husband, even though that's about to end. He did get me this nice ring." She held up her hand, showing off a beautiful silver ring with a dark green stone in the setting.

"Wow," Bud said. "That's something. Can I take a closer look, Melba?"

"Sure." She took off the ring and handed it to Krider, who examined it and then passed it on to Bud.

"Malachite," Bud noted. "Do you know where he got it?"

"Yes, I do," she answered. "He told me he found the stone right down there by the Slickrock Cafe. He took it into town and had one of Sonny's friends who's a silversmith make it into a ring. You know, Bud, I think he's trying, but he just can't seem to stop gambling. It's a Black Beast that's got him down and he can't get it off his neck."

"A Black Beast?" Krider asked with surprise, handing Melba back the ring.

"Yes, that's a term Jack always uses to describe things that are hard to do, a Black Beast."

"How long has he used that term?" Krider asked.

Melba looked puzzled. "Is there something wrong with it?"

"No, not at all," Krider tried to act nonchalant. "I like it."

"Oh, it's probably something he made up or maybe read when he was in college. He's used it forever."

"A bête noire," Krider replied, nodding at Bud. "What did he study in college?"

Melba filled their cups again from the percolator pot. "He used to be an English major. He never finished. Stanford University, out in California. Hard to believe, I know. His dad was a professor there and wanted him to be just like him, but Jack was a rebel. He took off, rode the rails, and came out here. Just like in some Steinway story, or is it Steinbeck? I dunno."

Bud whistled. "I'll be go to. Melba, Jack never told a soul about all this, not that I know of."

"I probably shouldn't mention it. He wanted to leave his past behind. He's never gone back, and as far as I know, never even talked to his dad, though he used to write his mom once in awhile until she passed away. He has a brother down in Texas at some university who stayed and did what his dad wanted. We've got letters several times from my sister that he's looking for Jack, but Jack won't ever contact him and my sister's under strict orders to not give out any information. Something about money due. But it doesn't matter. Me and Jack, we're done, finished like that old mare he fed baby food until she hit 30 and died. See, he has a kind heart, but it's this gambling..."

Bud thought about the diner, where Jack handed Sonny a big wad of bills. He'd assumed it was his owed wages, but maybe not. And then, there was Hans Rohr...

"Melba, we have to get going, but thanks for the coffee, and those are the best darn cookies I think I've ever had. Mind if I have another for the road?" Bud stood, putting his hand on Melba's shoulder.

"Take the whole bunch," she offered. "I got the recipe from Sonny's wife. I made them for Jack, and he couldn't be bothered to came home to eat them, so to hell with it." She stood and wrapped the cookies up in a napkin, handing them to Bud. "And Bud," she added, "That earring you've got makes you look handsome. Just like a pirate."

"Thanks," he replied, wincing. "And don't be too hard on the old guy. I don't think he could survive without you, in all honesty."

Bud and Krider were soon out the door and headed back down the road to try to find the Slickrock Cafe.

CHAPTER 14

As Bud approached the Arrowhead, he slowed down, expecting to see Jack's pickup parked there. It wasn't, but he stopped anyway, and he and Krider got out. They walked around, looking for tire tracks or anything that might be a clue to where Jack had gone. It didn't appear that anyone had stopped here since they were here last.

"Maybe he went up further onto the mesa," Krider offered.

"Probably," Bud replied. "I was hoping to figure out where the Cafe was, I know it's somewhere around here. But let's get on back into town. The day's wearing on, and I need to grab some paperwork before we head back to Green River."

They got back into the FJ and took off on down the road and were soon at the campground. It looked like the bikers were gone, though their tents were still there. Bud figured they'd gone on into town for supplies or to have dinner.

"Say, Prof," Bud said, "I forgot to mention something about that snake."

"What's that?"

"I have a theory that it was a plant. Someone was trying to scare the bikers off and put a big bullsnake in their camp, probably during the night. It's getting cold enough that they knew the snake would be immobile until it started to warm up today and the guys were up."

"Bud, how in heck would you know it's a plant?"

"Because it was the wrong color for up here. See, the bullsnakes up here have evolved a different color to blend in with the redrock. They have a bit of a pinkish tint to them—they're really beautiful. When I was in high school, some biologist came and studied them, and she gave a talk at our school about it. I've never forgotten that, and they really are different. That snake in their camp was just an ordinary bullsnake like you'd find out in the sagebrush flats."

"I'll be go to," Krider said. "Why would anyone want to do that?"

"Scare them off? I dunno, but my guess is that it has something to do with that Black Beast and those Malachites. It's all tied together."

"And maybe tied in with some kind of gambling thing Sonny Ottin has going?"

"Maybe," Bud replied. "Maybe involving Jack Pilling. Speak of the devil, and he appears." Bud nodded his head towards the campground entrance, where Jack's pickup sat. He pulled over next to it.

The driver's side door was hanging open, but there was no sign of Jack. Bud and Krider looked around a bit.

"He must have parked where we couldn't see him when we went up to his house. And there's his tracks," Krider pointed, "walking through the sand over there."

They followed the tracks down a narrow wash that led around through the campground and eventually turned towards the section where the bikers were camped.

Krider whispered to Bud, "I betcha anything he's hiding over there, up to some kind of mischief, if not worse. We might not want to just casually walk over there."

"You're right," Bud said. "Let's go back."

He and Krider returned to the FJ and got in. Bud then drove over to the bikers' camp and got out, motioning for Krider to follow, and then pulled his Ruger out of its holster under his jacket.

He started talking really loud, hoping Jack could hear him. He was now sure Jack was hiding nearby in the wash.

"Say, Deputy," Bud boomed out, "This is where that guy spotted that cougar. I bet it's over in the bushes, right over there." With that, Bud began taking pot shots in the general direction where he suspected Jack was, but intentionally aiming too high.

"Hold it! Hold it!" a voice boomed out.

No question, it was Whispering Jack.

"Who's out there?" Bud yelled. "This is the Sheriff. Come out with your hands up!"

Krider looked amused.

The voice replied, "Bud, it's me, Jack Pilling. Don't shoot!" They could now see a head sticking up out of the wash.

"Jack, for cryin' out loud, get outta there. There's a big cougar back in there."

The head now got taller, as Jack climbed the banks of the wash as fast as his rickety knees would carry him. He was soon by the pair, huffing and puffing. He had his rifle with him.

"Jack, what in hellsbells are you doing in that wash?"

Jack never lost a beat. "Huntin' that cougar," he grinned.

"Jack, you know those bikers will eat you alive. Every single one of them is armed to the teeth." Bud wasn't sure if that was true or not, but he guessed it could be.

"I was gonna spy on them, see what they're up to, Bud,

they're straight from the devil himself. Something you should be doing. I'm doing your job for you, and I ain't got no heath insurance like you do."

"You wouldn't need health insurance, Jack, that would be burial funds you'd be needing—or rather, Melba would need. And I'm quite capable of doing my job."

"Well, you should start doing it, then," Jack answered, testily.

"Alright, Jack, I'll do that. Hand over that rifle."

Krider stepped up from behind and took the rifle from Jack's hands, who was caught by surprise.

"It's a Browning, Bud. A Browning A-Bolt. Made right here in Utah," Krider informed him to the distant thunder of motorcycles approaching.

• • •

"Quick! Get in the FJ!" Bud told Jack, who obediently climbed in as Krider got in the back. They drove off before the bikers drove up, none the wiser that the trio had just been at their camp.

"Close call for you, Jack," Bud said, pulling up by Jack's pickup and letting the old man out. "I'm keeping this gun for awhile. The hospital room right next to Hum's is empty, and I want to keep it that way."

Jack looked shocked. "You can't keep my gun. That's unconstitutional. And watch how you hold it, the safety's broken."

"I'm keeping it for your own good, Jack. You can have it back in a day or two when these hombres are gone. Now you go on home. We were just up there visiting, and Melba sounds like she's pretty upset with you. She's planning on leaving. You need to go home and do some damage control."

"I already did. I bought her a ring. She won't go, she always says that."

"I think she means it this time—and she showed us the ring. Where exactly did you get that chunk of malachite?"

"Ain't sayin'." Jack was turning surly. "And I got two more rifles like that at home."

"Jack, where exactly is the Slickrock Cafe?" Krider asked.

Jack turned to Krider. "Ain't sayin' nuthin' to you, neither."

Krider grinned. "Talkin' must be your bête noire, eh?"

Jack looked surprised. "Whattya mean by that?"

"Your Black Beast," Krider answered.

For once, Whispering Jack was quiet. Without further ado, he got into his pickup and drove off.

CHAPTER 15

"Nice way to get the gun without telling Jack why," Krider commented. "Now we can check it out, see if the bullet came from it."

"True," Bud replied, "But he really shouldn't be armed. He's getting kind of goofy. I'm worried about him."

"You think he may be involved in all this?"

"It's a possibility," Bud answered.

Bud turned the FJ around and headed back to town. The cookies were wearing off fast, and he was thinking about getting a nice big hamburger down at the Uranium Diner.

That made him think of Wilma Jean. He needed to call her and see how things were going. Maybe it was time to get her to come down here with him and stay at Peggy Sue's, that way they could see each other once in awhile, which would be nice. He was starting to miss her good home cooking, too.

He and Krider drove by the campground, where the bikers were once again kicked back, smoking cigars and drinking beer and playing horseshoes. Bud wondered what their plans were and how long they would stay. He didn't really mind them being here, they'd been civil so far, for the most part, and they added a human element to a landscape that was generally pretty lonesome this time of year. But he wondered about that snake and why someone would put it there. He wondered if it had anything to do with the other strangeness going on.

Just then, Krider ended Bud's musing.

"Hey, stop, stop! Look over there, quick."

Bud pulled over, trying to see what had Krider so excited. Krider jumped out of the FJ, and Bud followed.

"What? What?" Bud asked.

"Look over there," Krider pointed to a fin that poked up behind another fin in the distance. "Where's your binoculars?"

Bud grabbed them from the FJ, popping off the lens caps and looking to where Krider pointed.

"What the heck?" Bud handed Krider the binoculars. "I must be hallucinating."

"No way!" Krider replied. "A llama?"

"Maybe someone's filming a cigarette commercial," Bud offered.

"That would be a camel, Bud, not a llama. It looks like it's alone, there's nobody leading it."

The llama disappeared behind the fin, and the pair stood there for a bit in wonder, then got back in the FJ and continued on down the hill in silence.

• • •

Bud pulled into the courthouse parking lot next to a big pink Lincoln. It looked just like Wilma Jean's, he noted, the one she'd won when she used to sell Mary Kay Cosmetics here in Radium. But what would she be doing down here? He had a sinking feeling she was looking for him.

Sure enough, two little heads popped up as Bud looked into the window. It was Pierre and Hoppie, who started barking madly while Pierre growled as if Bud were a badger. Bud patted the pair through the window, then he and Krider went on into the courthouse.

Wilma Jean was there, talking to Sandy, the dispatcher, who'd been in Wilma Jean's leagues when she owned Sinkhole Lanes here in Radium. She'd sold the business when Bud got the job as sheriff in Green River and they moved up there.

"Hi, Hon," Wilma Jean said to Bud. "Bet you're surprised to see me, huh?"

Bud sheepishly admitted he was.

"I've brought some clothes and stuff, and we're going to stay at Peggy Sue's for a bit. She needs our support, and I need my husband back again. Besides, I wanna go slumming." This was a little reverse joke she always used when they went to Radium, as the town was way more upscale than Green River.

"Howie's Maureen is taking care of things at home. She's quite the gal," Wilma Jean added.

Bud was relieved. Wilma Jean wasn't mad, and he was getting tired of driving back and forth to Green River. It would be nice to stay here for a bit, and it would give him more time to work on things, too.

Wilma Jean turned to Krider. "Peggy Sue has a guest room. I'm sure she wouldn't mind if you stayed there any time you wanted. She's a great hostess, Bill. She needs people around right now with all this happening to Hum."

Krider replied, "I really appreciate it, but right now I should probably get home and see my wife and girls. But I may take you up on that in the future, stay here a night or two, then go home for a bit, alternate."

"I really need your help on this case, Prof," Bud replied. "Why don't you take the FJ and go on back home, and I can use a patrol vehicle, then you come on back down when you can."

"Sounds good," Krider agreed. "I'll be in touch."

Bud handed Krider the keys and gave Wilma Jean a hug in passing.

• • •

Bud now sat in his office, fiddling with his ear-post, pondering what a llama might be doing up at Slickrock Flats, when someone tapped on the window in the door.

"Come in," Bud said.

In walked Deputy Hans Rohr. Seeing Bud, he stopped dead in his tracks, his face registering shock.

"Afternoon, Deputy," Bud said, motioning Hans to sit down. "What can I do for you?"

"You're our new sheriff?"

Hans wore a look on his face that said his days as a deputy for Radium were probably numbered.

"Last I heard, I am," Bud replied. "Unless Hum just got out of the hospital. What's up?"

"Um, er, I was going to ask if I could take a couple of days off. My wife's sick, and I really need to stay home and help her out. I'll take vacation time." He paused, then added, "Say, Sheriff, no hard feelings about the other day, I was just doing my job. You were going so slow I thought maybe you'd been drinking."

9 6

"No, no hard feelings at all, Hans. You can take the time off, and we'll do it as paid leave so you don't lose any vacation time."

Hans looked surprised. "Thank you, Sir," he answered.

Bud continued. "Hans, you have any idea why there would be llamas up at Slickrock? Anyone filming a commercial or anything?"

"Not that I know of," Hans answered, surprised.

"And Hans, you know anything about some illegal gambling that might be going on around town?"

Hans turned even paler than before. "No, Sir."

"OK. Say, Hans, I do have one little thing I want you to do when you're there at home, when you get time." Bud leaned back, opening his desk drawer. "I brought this from home just for you."

"I'd be glad to help out however I can," Hans said.

"Good, good," Bud replied. "Read this through, then when you get back, we'll take some time and discuss it pretty thoroughly. It's my duty as sheriff to ensure my deputies follow it."

"Sure, Sheriff," Hans said congenially.

Bud handed Hans a small hardbound book. Printed in gold on the front were the words "United States Constitution."

Hans blanched, thanked Bud, and walked out the door.

CHAPTER 16

Bud parked his sheriff's vehicle at the base of the Arrow-head and got out, Hoppie jumping out behind him. He checked the dog's collar and leash, making sure he couldn't pull out of it. He knew that Bassett hounds had only one master—their nose— and he wanted to be sure Hoppie couldn't get away from him. A hound dog running around out here following a scent could easily get lost, especially with the shadows lengthening as they now were.

He paused, then decided it would be prudent to call Krider and let him know what he was about to do. He dialed Krider's number.

Krider answered, "Bud, I was just getting ready to call you. Somebody's tailing me."

"Where are you?" Bud asked.

"I'm almost into Green River—I just got off the freeway. I need Howie's number. I want to call him."

"What does the vehicle look like?" Bud asked.

"It's a dark green car of some kind, a compact. Not really sure, as I don't want it to get too close. Two guys in it, Utah plates."

"How do you know they're following you?"

"I noticed them coming out of Radium, but they were holding back. Never thought they were following me, but

I took that back road coming around through B. Dalton Wells, and they took it, too, but way back. Then I decided to stop by the road awhile, and sure enough, when I pulled back on, I saw them way back there. They'd waited for me."

"OK, Prof, I don't want you in any danger. You head straight over to the sheriff's office and I'll call Howie. Whatever you do, don't go home, as they may be trying to figure out who you are."

"Roger."

Bud dialed Howie's cell phone.

"Sheriff Howie here."

"Howie, it's Bud. Listen, Bill Krider's coming into town as we speak, driving my FJ, and somebody's tailing him. He's coming straight to your office. Are you there?"

"No, I'm over at the Melon Rind, taking a break with Maureen."

"Howie, get over to the office. Pick Krider up and get him out of there, go someplace they can't follow and ditch them. We don't want whoever's following him to know where he lives."

"Roger, I'm on my way." Howie sounded excited.

Bud now called Krider back. "Prof, Howie's on his way. I have a feeling they think you're me. Whatever you do, don't go home until you're sure they're gone."

"What should I do?"

"Get into Howie's vehicle and have him take you someplace they can't follow."

"Like where?"

"You guys drive out the River Road and then take the old highway. It comes around by the airport and on out onto the Hanksville Road. It's a good thirty miles back around. They won't be able to follow you, it's too rough for a car. Just leave my FJ at Howie's office and have Howie take you home."

"I'm at his office right now, and here he comes."

"OK, Prof, be careful. Keep me posted. And Prof, the reason I was calling you is that I'm up at the Arrowhead as we speak, and I'm taking Hoppie down to the Porky Tree and see if we can find anything. I just thought someone should know where I'm at, and I don't want to worry Wilma Jean. Cal's not on duty or I'd tell him."

"Bud, it's almost dark."

"I know, but I have a theory, and it needs to be tested when there's not much light."

"OK, Bud, be careful. That car just stopped down the street a ways. Howie's here, so I'm going to hang up."

"Prof, try not to let them see who you are. I know they think you're me. If you can, get the plates. Howie should have a pair of binoculars."

"Roger," Krider replied, then hung up the phone.

• • •

Bud and Hoppie slowly started down the trail that led to the big Porky Tree and then on down into the quiet depths of Granstaff Canyon. Bud knew that Bassett hounds had a sense of smell second only to bloodhounds, and he'd been working with Hoppie a bit, thinking maybe he could train him to track. But he knew they had a long ways to go. But right now he had a theory, and he needed Hoppie to help him test it.

He knew it was risky coming down here alone, especially this time of day. The big fins were draped in shadow, only their tops lit by the slowly setting sun. They began to glow where the sunlight hit them at an oblique angle, and Bud once again wished he had a camera.

It then dawned on him that he did. He'd stuck the little pink Canon in his jacket pocket and forgot all about it. He pulled it out and took a few photos, trying to compose them in an artistic way, big fins with juniper trees in the foreground. He'd take a photo, then look at it on the LED screen, then take another.

He then turned and noticed the Salt Mountains were starting to take on alpenglow. He got so engrossed watching the sunset he almost forgot what he was there for, until Hoppie started pulling on him, wanting to go, then they started down the trail.

Bud thought again of the cougar carved into the rock and decided to go take a photo of it. They were soon there, and he was studying it, wondering who had carved it and why, when something caught his eye. Just around the corner from the cougar was another big rock, and Bud thought he could see carvings on it, also.

He wandered over to it and looked carefully. There was indeed another carving there, this one a huge snake that twisted and curled for a good three feet before it ended around the edge of the rock. Like the cougar, this somehow looked to Bud like it had an Incan influence. He studied it closely, and thought he could make out the marks of a little handheld battery-operated Dremel tool.

But he immediately lost interest in the carving when Hoppie started scratching at a small blackbrush—for what Bud then found made everything else seem minor in comparison.

There, half-hidden in the roots of the bush was what looked to be the end of a human finger bone. Bud carefully picked it up, placing it into a plastic baggie from his pocket. He then studied it, and what he saw struck him as very strange.

The bone wasn't grayish-white like one would expect, but was instead a rich green, as if it had been dipped in some kind of dye. Bud wondered if this, too, had been brought by a raven, and if so, where the rest of the skeleton was.

For some reason, he guessed he was looking at what could have something to do with the Malachites. He shivered, even though it was a warm evening, then turned and continued on down the trail.

After the detour, it didn't take long to reach the tree, and Bud looked all around again, hoping to find some clue as to what was going on. He thought about the llama, wondering again what would bring an animal like that up here. He hoped the Black Beast didn't have it for lunch, though he doubted that could happen, given his suspicions.

Hoppie was now pulling him, wanting to go over beyond the tree into the slickrock. Bud loosened his grip, following the little dog. Hoppie stopped at something that Bud at first thought was some kind of animal scat. He bent down to take a closer look.

Chewing tobacco! Didn't Melba say Jack Pilling had taken up chew? And it looked to be pretty fresh. Hoppie soon lost interest and started pulling back towards the tree.

By now it was nearly dark, and Bud began to feel uneasy. It was time to conduct his experiment. He again checked Hoppie's collar, then started yelling.

"Over here! Over here!"

He stopped and listened, watching Hoppie's ears. The little dog's hearing was far better than his, and Hoppie would warn him if anything were amiss.

Nothing. He began yelling again. "Malachite! Malachite! Over here!"

Now he could hear it, in the distance, the screaming. It sent a chill up his spine. Hoppie's ears went straight up, and the little dog looked surprised and scared.

"OK, Hoppie, now we run like hell," Bud said, taking off, the dog close behind.

The scream stopped, then started up again, the air vibrating. It then trailed off into the distance. Bud turned, and through the shadows, he could make out the same dark figure he'd seen when he first came out here to investigate Jimmy's murder.

It was coming at him fast, and he knew he couldn't outrun it, especially with Hoppie dragging behind. The little dog seemed unconcerned, even though Bud could see the Black Beast swiftly gaining on them.

He remembered the ledge where Pete, the hiker, had hid, and he ran for it. He was now practically dragging Hoppie along, and as he dived under, he felt for his Ruger, pulling it from its holster.

But Hoppie was still at the end of his lead, wanting to dawdle and sniff, and the little dog acted as if he definitely could see no reason to run. Bud tried to pull him under the ledge beside him, but he wouldn't come—he had no intention of getting in under that ledge. Bud called him, but Hoppie sat down on his haunches, a technique he'd used with great success any time he didn't want to go somewhere. If that didn't work, he would roll onto his back.

Bud began quickly crawling back out. He would have to carry the dog under the ledge with him. But just then, he looked up and there it was, only a mere twenty feet away, the Black Beast, and coming fast. Bud pointed his gun, ready to shoot, but it was too late. The Black Beast was on them.

CHAPTER 17

Bud tensed, waiting for the impact, but felt nothing.

He could then see Hoppie still sitting on his haunches as if nothing had happened.

Jumping up, Bud could see that the Black Beast had continued on up the trail, ignoring them completely.

His suspicions were right, he thought, standing up.

It wasn't real. It was some kind of projection, and a well-done one at that. He watched as it faded out into the shadows, gone.

But now he could hear something coming up the trail, and Hoppie's ears told him this was real. Someone was coming. He picked up the dog and carried him up into the slickrock, hiding in the shadows behind a juniper, holding Hoppie's mouth shut so he couldn't bark.

Whoever it was, he knew they were looking for him, and there was no way he was going to let them find him. He knew this area better than anyone on earth, and he knew exactly where to go to get through the big fins without hitting dead ends or getting rimrocked.

Bud quickly and silently headed back into the fins, carefully watching so he wouldn't stumble. His night vision wasn't that good, but it was still dusk, and he could see a little. But when things got pitch black, he wanted to be out of there.

He now let Hoppie down and continued on, passing a big pour-over. He was in a wide wash, and he knew it was the one that drained down into Granstaff Canyon from the Arrowhead. He could follow it right up to his truck and be there in less than 15 minutes.

He started up the wash, then realized that whoever was looking for him would beat him to the truck and probably lay out an ambush. He couldn't go back that way. But where to go? It was a long walk back into town, and the only way back down the cliffs was along the road. And there he would be easy prey.

Then it occurred to him—he would go to the campground and ask the bikers for help. They would get him out of this pickle.

He crossed the wash, heading through a sagebrush flat, trying to hide behind the scattered juniper trees. Now he was at the road. He crossed, angling back across the slickrock in the general direction of the campground.

Suddenly, Hoppie stopped and started growling. Bud's heart jumped, and he pulled out his Ruger. Whoever it was, they had caught up with him. It was now dark enough that he couldn't see much, just shadowy shapes and forms.

Now Bud made out a hint of movement a mere thirty feet or so away. He held his gun up to his eye, ready to shoot. Whatever it was saw him move, let out a yip, then turned and ran in the other direction. A coyote!

Bud sighed, then turned and continued on towards the campground, Hoppie close behind. To Bud's knowledge, Hoppie had never seen a coyote, and he was now fully ready to follow at whatever pace Bud wanted, tail between his legs.

Bud could soon hear voices and see a campfire. The bikers were yelling and enjoying themselves, probably drinking, and he hoped he didn't get shot when he made his appearance.

He stood in the same wash as Jack Pilling had earlier and watched as the bikers seemed to be playing some kind of Russian Roulette. A small gun was making the rounds, and each person would in turn hold it to their head and pull the trigger.

Bud grimaced. He had hoped they had more sense than that. He wondered if death by Russian Roulette would be considered suicide or murder by peer pressure. As the gun made the rounds, so did several bottles.

Bud just stood and watched, not sure what to do, until the gun finally went off. It made a popping sound and the burly biker holding it to his head appeared to fall over dead. Everyone laughed and cheered with great gusto.

But to Bud's surprise, the dead biker then stood and took what looked like bills from his pocket, placing them into a jar in the center. He then stood back, out of the game.

Bud grinned. They were playing a form of low-stakes poker, using a cap gun. They had to be drunker than skunks to consider that entertaining.

He was ready to climb the bank of the wash and step into the firelight when his phone rang. He could see from the caller ID that it was Howie. He quickly shut off the ringer, but not quickly enough.

The bikers all jumped to their feet, kicking back chairs and scattering, spilling bottles and cans. Before Bud could say siccum, Barry was standing over him, gun drawn, motioning for him to come out of the wash, while Hoppie hid behind him, growling.

• • •

"Don't shoot!" Bud said. "I'm one of you." He pulled on his earlobe, showing off the ear-post.

Barry grinned and put away the gun. He turned to the gang.

"It's OK, boys, it's just our snake-handling sheriff."

Someone muttered that things were going to hell in a handbasket when Barry would say it was OK cause it was just the sheriff.

Soon everyone went back to drinking and partying, paying Bud no mind. Everyone except the gang leader, Barry.

"Come on and join the party, Sheriff," Barry said. "And explain why you're spying on us."

"I wasn't spying," Bud explained, stepping into the firelight, pulling Hoppie along behind him. "I was just out walking the dog."

Barry guffawed. "Walking the dog, in the dark, down the wash that goes behind an armed motorcycle gang's camp? More like walking the Grim Reaper."

Bud grinned, then added, "You guys aren't as scary as you might like to be. But Barry, I need your help. Somebody's been following me. I headed this way cause I was afraid to go back to my truck. They were ahead of me and could be waiting to ambush me there."

Barry replied, "I'm confused. Someone was stalking you, but they were ahead of you? What were they, walking backwards?"

"No, they were behind me, but I ditched them and they got ahead of me."

"Well, why didn't you just shoot them and be done with it?"

"C'mon, you know I wouldn't operate like that. I might hurt someone."

Barry laughed again. "What do you want me to do, go shoot them for you?"

"No, I need a ride back to my vehicle. And cover."

"Let me see if I understand this, Sheriff. You're asking the leader of a biker gang to cover for you?"

"Yup," Bud affirmed. "I could deputize you. Actually, what would be even better is if you went and got my patrol truck and brought it back. That way I wouldn't have to leave Hoppie here."

He wasn't sure the gang would look after the little dog properly in their drunken state, and Hoppie might try to follow him if he left. There was no way he could take the dog along on the back of a motorcycle.

"I get it. We go back and take the heat on your behalf. What if we get shot?" Barry asked.

"Then you could sue the sheriff's department, I guess—assuming you lived. Not that we have any money."

Barry laughed again. "I dunno, Sheriff. Would it be legal for me to drive your sheriff's truck?"

"As long as you had my permission," Bud replied. "And the keys."

Barry paused, then said, "Tell you what. I'll do it if you'll take my picture driving it and email me a copy, along with a certificate saying I'm officially a deputy."

"You're on," Bud replied, handing Barry the keys, wondering what in the heck he was thinking.

CHAPTER 18

Barry and Jeff had taken off on Jeff's motorcycle, leaving Bud to think about whether he had made a good decision or not. He didn't figure anyone would shoot at them or bother them, and Barry wasn't drunk, so Bud figured it would all work out. He himself seemed to be the one the stalker was after. This made him remember that someone had been tailing Krider and that Howie had been trying to call him.

Bud pushed the callback button on his phone, and Howie answered.

"Sheriff, where you been? We're stuck out here and need help."

"Sorry, Howie, I got into a bit of a bind," Bud answered, not mentioning that his phone ringing was what had helped get him there. "What's going on?"

"We're out here and hit a pothole and had a flat. I just had one already this morning, and the tire's in the shop getting fixed. And that means we don't have a spare."

"Isn't there anyone a bit closer that you could call? It'll take me a good hour or more to get there. Did you ditch whoever was following Krider?"

"It appears so. We're out on the old highway, and it's full of potholes like I've never seen. The county should be maintaining it a bit better."

"It's been abandoned for years, Howie, ever since they built the new road."

Howie added, "I don't know anybody that would come out here, all these potholes make it slow going. Maureen would, but she's driving a little VW bug and would never make it. And Bill Krider would, but he's stuck out here with me. I need to hire a deputy. I've been telling the mayor that ever since you left, but he doesn't think we can afford it."

Bud sighed. It was going to be a long night. He noted the last lingering sunrays were now gone and the stars were coming out. Orion was poking its head above the eastern horizon.

"I'll be there as soon as I can, Howie. What size tire you need, and what's the bolt configuration?"

There was a moment of silence, then, "16 with five lugs."

"Perfect," Bud replied. "You can use the spare off my FJ. I'll stop and get it, then come out. How far out there are you?"

"About five miles past the airport. But Bud, somebody may be watching that FJ, waiting for you to come back. You might not wanna go there."

"You're right, Howie. I'll figure something else out and be there soon."

"10-4 and over," Howie said, hanging up the phone.

• • •

Bud was back in his own element again, driving back down the Slickrock Flats road into town, Hoppie by his side.

Barry and Jeff had retrieved his truck and brought it back without incident, and Bud had taken a variety of photos of Barry standing by the vehicle and sitting inside it with the lights flashing.

The gang had commented on the color of his camera, then decided they wanted a photo with everyone standing around the patrol truck, and that had evolved into a photo shoot with the bikers on their motorcycles surrounding the truck while Bud was in it, lights flashing, Jeff taking the pictures. It had turned out to be quite the photo shoot, and Bud was glad he wouldn't be the sheriff for long, as otherwise he might not be the sheriff for long if word got out.

He was tired, and now he had to go get Howie and Krider. Maybe he'd just spend the night up in Green River so he wouldn't have to drive back.

As he drove down the steep switchbacks into town, he suddenly steered into the other lane to miss a dark figure walking on the road—someone leading some kind of animal. He turned on his flashing lights for safety, then pulled over as far as he could and got out.

He walked up to the figure. "Hey there, you're living dangerously—are you aware that nobody can see you?" As he spoke, the flashing lights lit up the figure's face, and he thought he recognized the eyes, but couldn't be sure, as whoever it was had a full-face beard.

Now that Bud could see better, he noted that the figure was dressed like someone from Peru, in a woven red poncho decorated with intricate designs that featured snakes and cougars, a woven wool hat, and dark knee-length pants and sandals.

But of greater interest to Bud, the man was leading, of all things, a llama.

The man just shrugged, saying nothing. For some reason, Bud got the idea that whoever it was didn't want Bud to know.

Bud wasn't sure what to say. He wanted to ask the man what he was doing up here with a llama, but he really no authority to ask unless he could give a good reason for asking, which he couldn't.

"Look, I'd hate to see you get hit, so I'm gonna escort you until you get down off here."

With that, Bud followed him down the switchbacks with his lights flashing for safety. Once off the switchbacks, the man got back onto the side of the road, where he could walk safely the rest of the way into town.

Bud now passed the man and headed on down. He had no idea what was going on, and he was too tired to even care at this point.

Here was some guy, dressed like a Peruvian, walking down the road in the dark, leading a llama, probably the same llama he and Krider had seen earlier. It was all too much, and Bud just wanted to go back to his bungalow in Green River and have Wilma Jean waiting with a nice fried chicken dinner.

He was regretting his choice in taking this job—it was starting to remind him of the burnout he'd felt before he quit up in Green River. And he had nothing to show for it so far—he wasn't a bit closer to solving anything than he'd been the afternoon he was sitting on that tractor up at Krider's Melon Farm and the call had come from Peggy Sue, telling him about Hum.

Now back in town, Bud stopped by Peggy Sue's, where Wilma Jean's big Lincoln was parked in the driveway. The house was a nice ranch-style rambler, and he recalled many pleasant evenings spent there with Hum and Peggy Sue, back when he and Wilma Jean lived in Radium. He wondered if Hum was doing any better.

He dropped Hoppie off, then told Wilma Jean what was going on. She laughed ironically when he told her he was probably going to spend the night at the bungalow in Green River, but she didn't seem to mind, as she and Peggy Sue were getting ready to go to a movie.

Bud stopped at the tire shop and got a used spare just before they closed, throwing it in the back of his truck. He was hungry, so he stopped and grabbed a to-go burrito from the Wrangler gas station on the edge of town and was soon on his way, driving towards the dark horizon, thinking about Black Beasts, biker gangs, Incan petroglyphs, and llamas, trying once again to make sense of it all.

CHAPTER 19

Bud pulled off the freeway and onto the highway that led into Green River. He was now very aware of any other vehicles on the road, wondering who had followed Krider and why. He knew they must still be around, trying to figure out where Krider had gone, except he suspected they thought Krider was him.

He pulled into the Eastwinds Truck Stop, just a half-block from the sheriff's office. He could make out his FJ parked down the street, the flickering street light making the tan color look yellow. He sat for a bit, watching, and then, just as he was ready to go, he noticed a dark green car coming down the street from behind him. He could make out two people in it, and as it came to the FJ, it slowed down, then continued on.

The car headed down the street, then turned around and came back, pulling into the alley across the street from the FJ and next to Howie's Cafe. It then turned out its lights.

Dang it, thought Bud, wishing he had someone to give him backup. He wanted to go over and see what they were doing, get some ID and run the plates. But there was no way he was going alone, especially since he knew they were looking for him.

He radioed the State Trooper's office, but nobody answered. They had an office here in Green River, but it wasn't manned at night. He tried again, finally getting through, but the trooper that answered was way over on the Swell and couldn't be of any help.

Bud sat there for awhile, wondering what to do. He wanted those plates, at the very least, so he could maybe figure out who it was. Then he needed to get out to Krider and Howie and help them. They were probably wondering where he was. He began to fiddle with his ear-post.

Bud figured that whoever it was probably wouldn't suspect he was nearby in a Radium sheriff's pickup, so maybe he could take them by surprise. He slowly pulled out of the gas station, then turned and went around the block, coming up around the corner from where they waited in the alley, cutting his lights before they could see him.

He parked the truck, then slipped out, touching the Ruger in its shoulder holster. Like someone in a spy movie, he carefully made his way up the side of the alley, using the shadows along the buildings for cover. He was soon close enough to read the plates, and he took a little notebook from his pocket, writing the number down.

Mission accomplished, but should he now try to get a closer look, see who it was? He knew it was risky, but he decided he would.

He slipped a little closer. He could make out nothing but the backs of two heads, but soon one of the heads turned to where he could see by the streetlight.

Bud couldn't believe his eyes.

It was Melba Pilling.

Now the driver was rolling down the window, and he soon spat something out. A slight breeze blew a pungent odor back to Bud.

It was the smell of chewing tobacco.

● ● ●

Bud dearly wanted to tap on their car window and ask them what they were doing, but something said not to—maybe it was the inflection in Jack's voice when Bud had taken his rifle, plus him reminding Bud that he had two more like it at home.

Bud silently snuck back down the alley, got into his truck, and headed on out to the airport. They could just sit there all night, he thought, irritated at them for doing whatever they were doing, sitting there, stalking him.

Just before the airport, he turned left onto another road and drove on into the dark. This road was the old highway, the main and only route from Green River to the small desert town of Hanksville until sometime in the 1960s, when a new road was built, bypassing this one. Now it saw use only from an occasional local who used it as a shortcut and was willing to risk the numerous potholes, as well as risk the dangerous culverts that were on the verge of caving in. It eventually connected with the new highway, and one could go on to Hanksville or make a big loop back to Green River, eventually meeting the freeway.

Bud drove slowly, steering around the potholes, some so deep he knew if he went into them he would never get back out. Finally, he could see the tail lights of another vehicle reflecting in his headlights.

He pulled up behind Howie's Toyota Land Cruiser, which had a jack under one side and a tire by the road. Howie and Krider were leaning against the vehicle, but when they saw Bud, they ran up to him, and they soon had the tire out of his truck and were putting it on. Everyone was eager to get home.

Tire changed, Krider rode with Bud, following Howie. Bud would take Krider home, then get his FJ tomorrow. Before long, they were on the freeway, headed back towards Green River and could see the town's lights twinkling off in the distance.

Bud told Krider about everything that had happened that day, hoping he would have some insight into things, but they were both tired and uninspired. Back in town, they watched carefully to see if anyone were following, but saw no one. Bud dropped Krider off and was soon pulling into his own drive, the lights of the bungalow off, making the place seem lonely and desolate.

Bud unlocked the kitchen door and turned on the light, half expecting Pierre to jump from behind the door and grab his pant leg while Hoppie barked madly. But the dogs were in Radium with Wilma Jean, and all was quiet.

He took off his coat and holster, putting his gun into the safe, then checked the refrigerator. There was plenty to eat, but it all had to be cooked, and he didn't feel like cooking. The burrito he'd grabbed in Radium wasn't setting too well with him, so he ate some Tums, made himself a cold ham and cheese sandwich, and kicked back in his easy chair.

He turned on the TV, channel surfing for a bit, then turned it back off. Nothing interested him. The house seemed desolate, nothing like it normally did. He got up and made sure all the doors were locked and the curtains pulled, then took his gun back out of the safe and placed it by his chair.

He finally called Wilma Jean, but she didn't answer. They must still be at the movie, he thought. He got up, looked again in the fridge, made himself a bowl of vanilla bean ice cream, and sat back down, turning the TV back on.

He watched a little bit of an old rerun of "I've Got a Secret" where some guy was dressed up like a monkey to fool the contestants, but that soon ended and he was back to channel surfing.

Finally, he turned the TV off and picked up the book he'd been working on for several weeks, trying to wade through at Wilma Jean's request. It was the latest bestseller, all about how to get rich just by thinking about it, and he knew it would never work. But he tried his best to read it. It was called, "How to Get More Living out of Life and Get Rich in the Meantime."

He was at the section called, "Five Rules for Freeing Your Creative Machinery." He found where he'd marked his place and started reading.

1. *Do your worrying before you place your bet, not after.*
2. *Always respond to the present moment.*
3. *Try to do only one thing at a time.*
4. *Relax while you work.*
5. *Sleep on it.*

Bud put the book down. He would think about these points for awhile, absorb them. He got up and took the blue striped afghan Wilma Jean had made from the back of the couch, sitting back down and wrapping it around him.

He closed his eyes to think. "Relax while you work," he thought. Yup, that was easy to do when you were hunting down a murderer and being chased by huge black cougars or jaguars or whatever it had been.

"Do only one thing at a time. Sleep on it."

Before he knew it, Bud had gone to sleep, snoring lightly with his head tilted back and twitching a bit, just like Pierre when he was chasing wabbits in his sleep.

CHAPTER 20

Bud stood at the Porky Tree where Krider had found the malachite, listening. He thought he could hear someone yelling, or was it just the wind? No, it was over there, far in the distance, someone was yelling for help. It sounded a bit like Krider.

He checked his Ruger, making sure it was loaded, then put it into his coat pocket where he could rest his hand right on it. Now the breeze had changed a bit, and yes, someone was definitely calling for help. They now sounded desperate.

Bud felt a chill go down his back, that same chill he always felt when he was getting into a dangerous situation. He knew he should turn back, go home. Wilma Jean would be waiting with something good for dinner. This was a trap.

But it sounded just like Krider. He had to go, his friend needed him. What kind of person would run away when someone needed his assistance? Only a coward could ignore that plea.

He headed down the old stock trail that led into Granstaff Canyon. He tried to be unobtrusive, but there was really no way he could hide. He soon reached the edge of the canyon, where the trail started to switchback straight down the canyon wall. The voice was down there, still calling, sounding even more desperate. And yes, it was definitely Krider.

He carefully started down the trail, which now cut through slickrock, into the canyon. This one section, a thick ledge, had blocked the trail, keeping the cowboys from being able to drive their stock down to the creek at the bottom of the canyon, so they'd blasted it out with dynamite.

The slickrock lived up to its name—one had to watch their step, or they would slip and slide down down down, not stopping until they reached the bottom.

When he'd come up here as a kid, Bud had seen the occasional skeleton of some unfortunate steer who had, in its thirst, misjudged the steepness and tumbled into the canyon depths. He'd heard of a cowboy who had also died here, his horse losing its footing, but he wasn't sure who it had been.

He slowly and carefully walked down the slickrock until the trail became deep sand and wasn't as treacherous.

Now the voice was closer, and Bud could tell it wasn't down in the bottom of the canyon after all. He stopped warily, trying to discern where it was coming from. The breeze shifted, making the voice also shift, and it now sounded like it was coming from just around the corner, where the trail paralleled the canyon wall for a bit.

Bud carefully slipped around the corner, watching for anything that could be a trap. But what he saw instead was a large alcove, its maw going deep into the cliff with a blackness his eyes couldn't penetrate. He hesitated, but again he heard Krider calling for help, now calling Bud's name. Krider was in the alcove.

Bud's instincts said not to go, but his empathy overrode them. He had to help Krider. He started into the alcove, gun in hand.

Now all was silent, and Krider called no more. Bud couldn't see into the thick blackness. He stopped and stood there, wondering what to do.

Suddenly, with no warning, something grabbed him from behind, knocking his gun to the ground. He could feel its fingers, and they were cold as ice and dug into his neck like bones as they pushed him along. He was helpless.

Soon, they were deep into the alcove, where Bud could barely make out a glowing light, like a firefly, but a pale icy blue. As he stood, watching it, a strange feeling came over him—he felt cold and like he was turning into stone, the purest greenest stone imaginable.

Now the light began to glow stronger and brighter, and he could see his hands. They were pure green, the same beautiful dark color as the malachite Krider had found, like the malachite in Melba's ring. He began to feel even colder, an icy cold like the bony hands that dug into his neck.

Now the light grew and lit the entire alcove, and he could see strange symbols and writings on its walls. The same Incan cougar he and Bill had seen carved into the rocks above was here, only larger, and a huge carved snake curled around the alcove and disappeared around the corner.

The icy hands were no longer on Bud's neck, and he turned to meet his assailant.

What he saw made his blood run cold. There, backlit by the strange blue glow, were two skeletons, but they were somehow alive. One had the tip of its little finger missing. They stared at him with empty eye sockets. Bud wanted to run, but was frozen.

Finally, one of them spoke. "It's no mystery where we are, you know the place well—it's the Slickrock Cafe. But be very wary, for there are those who would kill you for searching for us. We want to go home, we're very tired."

With that, the glow grew until it also lit them from the front. Bud could see that both skeletons were encrusted with beautiful green stones.

It was the Malachites.

• • •

Bud woke himself moaning, and he sat there for a bit, disoriented and afraid. He got out of the chair, feeling like he had just been the main character in some horror movie. He didn't care much for such and never watched them. He knew what being scared felt like, and he didn't like it one bit. It was bad enough facing danger in real life, but doing it in his sleep was a bit much.

He wondered what the dream had meant. He wasn't much of one for dream analysis, figuring dreams were just the brain exercising itself without the restraint normally provided by the conscious brain. But he did believe that sometimes one's subconscious would try to tell them something through dreaming. He'd learned that in his previous case.

He didn't like this feeling one bit, and he wished Wilma Jean and the dogs were here. He hated to admit it, but everything seemed spooky without them.

He got up and wandered around a bit, then made a decision. Without further ado, he got his gun and holster, put on his coat, turned out the lights, locked the door, and headed back down to Radium.

In one hour, he would be with his wife and the dogs, and all would be well.

CHAPTER 21

Bud sat in his office, wondering why Jack and Melba Pilling would follow his FJ to Green River. He'd had Cal run the plates, and they'd come back as definitely belonging to the couple. He just couldn't picture Jack being foolish enough to shadow him because he was mad about Bud taking his rifle, nor Melba going along with it. It just didn't make sense.

But what really didn't make sense was the dream he'd had last night. It was still bothering him, and he kept going over it, trying to figure out if he were subconsciously aware of some clues his conscious mind was blocking for some reason.

Could it be that he knew where the Slickrock Cafe was all along and didn't realize it? Was it some place he'd been to as a kid and didn't connect as being the Cafe?

Jack Pilling knew where it was, but he wasn't talking, and at this point, Bud wasn't sure he wanted to go back up there to see when Jack would start talking. Taking a man's rifle was second in these parts only to taking his food and water. Heck, Bud thought, maybe it wasn't even second—if you had a rifle, you could get food and water.

The rifle was now at the forensics lab to see if it were the same one that had fired the bullet that had killed Jimmy. Bud sincerely hoped it wasn't.

He'd received a message earlier in the morning from Krider telling Bud he was going to spend the day at home, but would go get Bud's FJ and take it to the bungalow for him. Bud was kind of glad, as he needed some time alone to think, even though one couldn't ask for a better partner than Krider. It was just the nature of the business, you had to stop and think, Bud thought.

Bud now kicked his feet up on his desk, leaning back in his chair, and wondered about the mysterious man leading the llama. He had no idea who or what that was about, but wondered if it might have something to do with the Peruvian-Incan theme that seemed to be invading Slickrock Flats.

Now Bud remembered a call he needed to make. He dialed the number.

"Radium Memorial. How may I direct your call?"

"Doctor McAllister, please."

Bud was put on hold and listened to what some might call music for a bit, then a voice answered.

"Doctor McAllister."

"Hello, Doctor, this is Bud Shumway, Interim Sheriff replacing Hum Stocks. I have a few questions, if you have time to answer them."

"Sure, Sheriff, shoot away."

"First, how's Hum doing? Any change?"

"Well, yes, he seems to be breathing better, and his heart is now regular, whereas he had a bit of arrhythmia before. But he's still in a deep sleep."

"Did his wife tell you he spoke to me when I was in there a few days ago?"

"Yes, she did, and that's definitely a good sign. As for prognosis, I personally think he's going to come to and be fine, especially since he talked to you and seems to have his speech and cognitive abilities unimpaired. It's just a matter of time. I've seen these types of head injuries before, and the body just needs to sleep them off. It's a form of mild coma."

"Well, I hope you're right. Say, he's got to be getting hungry by now, wouldn't you think?"

"No, he's on an IV."

"I know, but what I mean is, the smell of food might be a really good thing now to help him wake up. He's like me, he likes to eat."

"Not a bad idea," the doctor answered.

Bud continued, "But I need to ask, were you the doctor that saw him when he first came in? Did you treat the original injury?"

"Yes, I did."

"Did you find anything that might be evidence of what he was hit with?"

"Well, no, I'm not sure he was hit. He might have fallen."

Bud paused. "You know, Hum's a very competent outdoorsman, and he's very agile. I really can't picture him falling. He would've had to land pretty hard to get a blow like that, wouldn't he?"

"Yes, but it is possible—if he hit his head just right."

"But it would be more logical to assume an injury like that was from being assaulted, wouldn't it, Doctor?"

"That doesn't mean he was, Sheriff. The jury's still out."

"OK, but is it alright for me to come and visit him?"

"No, he still isn't ready for visitors. He's not awake. I'm sorry."

"You going to be there in a bit, Doctor, I mean just in case I were to come down, maybe stop by and say hello?"

"No, I'm going into a staff meeting here in about 10 minutes."

"OK. Thanks, you've been a great help."

"My pleasure, Sheriff."

• • •

Bud was soon at the hospital, where he casually walked into Hum's room. There was no one there besides Hum, which he had suspected might be the case, and he decided to make the best of it while he could.

Hum's color seemed much better than last time he'd been here, and he was breathing normally, just like the doc had said. Bud leaned over Hum's bed.

"Hey, Hum, it's Bud. How ya doin', Buddy?"

There appeared to be a bit of motion under one of Hum's eyelids, but Bud wasn't sure. Bud continued.

"Hum, I've been all over since I was here last, trying to find out who killed Jimmy and who whacked you on the head. But I'm stuck."

He paused, thinking he heard footsteps coming, but it was a false alarm.

"Hum, I'm not supposed to be in here, but I need to know, where the hell's the Slickrock Cafe?"

Bud now definitely saw motion under one eyelid. He hoped Hum would wake up and talk again, and this time he would try to keep him awake. He waited patiently.

After awhile, he started talking to Hum again, pretty sure he wasn't going to wake up this time.

"Hum, we're staying over at your place. It's sure nice. It reminds me of the good old days when me and Wilma Jean lived here. Remember that time we all had the barbecue out at Slickrock Flats and we nearly got run over by that cattle drive..."

Bud stopped. A flicker of light was entering his consciousness. Barbecue...cattle drive... Slickrock Cafe...

Bud jumped up."Hum, I know it. If it was a snake it would've bit me. Dammit Hum, wake up! I think I know where that damn Cafe is after all. It's Lost Park, isn't it? I can't believe I didn't see it before. You turn there by the Porky Tree, that's why it seemed familiar."

Bud saw Hum's finger twitch, but he couldn't wait, he now had to leave—someone was coming.

"OK, Hum, I'll be back. You stay outta trouble, Buddy."

Bud squeezed Hum's hand, then took off out the door, passing a nurse on the way. She didn't notice which room he'd come from, as she was too busy studying Hum's chart, wondering why the doctor had ordered that Hum get a steak dinner every evening, even though he obviously couldn't eat it.

CHAPTER 22

Bud pulled up to Jimmy Ottin's rock shop, parking next
to the antique 1950s drill rig that set next to an even older
Army truck with "Kilroy" painted on the side. Out front of
the shop were several big tables loaded to the gills with
rocks of all shapes and sizes. One table said "Utah" on it,
another said "Dinosaur Bone," and another had no sign at
all, a mishmash of rocks of all sizes and varieties.

He stopped at the dino bone table, thinking of all the
times he and Sonny had gone bone hunting with Jimmy. Of
course, back then it wasn't against the law to collect verte-
brate fossils, or maybe it was and they didn't know it, but
even if it were, Jimmy wouldn't have let a simple thing like
that get in the way.

Jimmy had found some great finds out in the deserts
around Radium and Green River, and he'd even found
a unique species of dinosaur, which was then named after him, the Camasaurus ottini. He had been very proud
of that, and had photos of the find hung all over the rock
shop.

Bud was jolted back into the present when a voice
informed him, "It's all legal, Sheriff. Collected on private
lands."

He looked up to see a skinny blonde guy who was maybe all of twenty years old looking at him suspiciously. He looked enough like Sonny to be his brother. The kid continued, "Looking for anything in particular?"

"Is Sonny here?" he asked.

"Nope," came the reply.

"Any idea when he'll be back?"

"Nope."

"Mind if I go inside and look around?" Bud asked.

"Nope."

Bud grinned. The kid had to be an Ottin. Surly as he was, Bud already liked him—Sonny had been just like him at that age.

Bud went into the shop and looked around, reminiscing, recalling the many summer days he'd hung out here with the Ottin family, all the trips out rock hounding, and Jimmy's innate dislike of government in any form and constant railing on that subject.

All the while, the blonde kid watched him like a hawk. Bud was ready to leave when something caught his eye— a whole shelf dedicated to chunks of malachite! Probably from the Blue Jay Pit, he surmised.

"Where's this from?" he asked.

"Blue Jay Pit. There's some nice stuff there if you're looking for something for your gal. Makes nice jewelry." Bud was surprised at how talkative the kid had suddenly become. He figured he must work on commission.

"You sell much of this?" he asked.

"Dunno. Sonny just brought it in this morning."

"Say, I didn't catch your name," Bud said. "I'm Bud Shumway." He held out his hand.

The kid shook it, but barely. He replied, "I'm Tommy Ottin."

"You Sonny's cousin? I grew up with Sonny."

This simple statement had an immediate effect. Tommy changed into an entirely different person, becoming the model of congeniality.

"You did?" Tommy asked. "You're that Bud? Oh, man, I've heard a lot about you and your escapades with Sonny. Aren't you the one who painted over the R?"

Bud grinned. "That would be me."

"And now you're the sheriff?"

"Just temporarily, until Hum gets better. But I didn't know Sonny had other family here."

"I haven't been here that long. I came down from Salt Lake to get away from my stepmom. I was working over at Red River by Night but I got laid off, so Sonny said I could come help him out. His dad was my uncle."

"Red River by Night?" Bud asked. "I rode that once with my niece, Mindy. Man, they crammed us and about 50 tourists into this boat and nobody had a life jacket or anything, then we took off at dusk motoring up the river. When we got up there a ways, the boat turned around and we slowly floated back down while some guy narrated this campy thing about the Old West and I worried about hitting a sandbar. Some guys followed along on the highway by the river, lighting up the canyon walls and projecting huge corny pictures of cowboys and Indians and stuff."

Tommy replied, "Yeah, that was my job, to light up the walls. My friend drove the truck. It has all these huge lights and I made them hit the right places as we drove along. It was pretty fun."

133

"I bet. Well, nice to meet you, Tommy. Tell Sonny I stopped by, will you?"

"You bet," came the reply.

"Oh, and I want to buy this piece here," Bud said, holding up a beautiful chunk of malachite the size of a quarter and bearing a sticker with the price of $25.

Tommy looked surprised. "I never even saw you pick that up."

"A little trick I learned from your uncle," Bud grinned, putting several bills on the counter.

• • •

Bud was thinking about going on up to Slickrock Flats when his phone rang. It was Cal.

"Sheriff, we're having a bit of a problem with some bikers from that gang camped up the hill. They're in the Uranium Diner demanding that they be served beer with their meal, and you know this is Utah, you can't just be served beer like that. I'm worried it's going to explode, and so is Willy, the owner."

"Do they understand that they have to join the Uranium Diner private club first?"

"I told them all that, but they have to be sponsored to join, and nobody wants to sponsor them."

"Is Barry there? He's the big guy who always wears a red bandanna, has both ears pierced. He's their leader."

"Yes, there's a guy here like that."

"OK, Cal. You go tell Willy that I'm sponsoring Barry, and after Barry's in, he can sponsor another guy and on down the line. That should work."

Cal was silent. Finally, he asked, "Did I hear that right?

You're going to sponsor this biker gang leader so they can all get in there and drink? It isn't even mid-afternoon yet."

"That's right, Cal. Better them drinking in the restaurant there where we can keep an eye on them than out somewhere where we can't. It's only 3.2 beer anyway."

"You got a point there," Cal conceded.

"It'll work out OK," Bud assured him, then hung up, changing his mind about Slickrock Flats and heading instead out to the Radium Airport.

CHAPTER 23

Bud pulled into the parking lot next to the airplane hangers. He looked around a bit until he saw an old white Ford pickup, then parked and got out. Tim was here, at least his truck was, Bud thought, hoping the pilot wasn't out flying tourists around.

He proceeded to Hanger 3, where he knew Tim kept his four-passenger Cessna, hoping he would be there. He peeked into the hanger, and sure enough, Tim was there, working on his plane. He put his tools down and greeted Bud when he saw who it was.

"Bud Shumway! Long time no see, pard," Tim shook hands warmly with Bud. "But what's this lawman's uniform? You sheriff now? I thought you quit."

"I did," Bud replied. "But now I'm sheriff here, but just until Hum gets better."

"What's wrong with Hum?"

"He got whacked on the head. But say, Tim, how much would you charge me to fly up Granstaff Canyon and over Slickrock Flats? I need to do some recon work out there."

"Well, I guess it would depend on how long you wanted to fly around."

"I'm thinking we could probably do it in an hour, but it might be a bit longer," Bud replied. "I'm going to let the sheriff's office pay for it, since it's official business."

"I usually charge about $100 an hour."

"When could we go?" Bud asked.

"We could go right now. I was just doing a little mainte-nance, but it can wait, nothing important. Give me a couple of minutes to put everything away, and I'll be ready."

Bud knew Tim kept his plane in perfect condition, and he also had the reputation of being the best pilot in the re-gion. That only made sense, as his dad was Winn Wells, one of the canyon country's pioneer pilots, flying early uranium prospectors around the canyons. Winn had many a wild tale told about his piloting abilities, and Tim followed in his footsteps.

"Sounds good to me," Bud replied.

• • •

They were soon in the air, Tim piloting the plane with an ease that was second nature.

"How long you been flying?" Bud asked. They were both wearing headphones so they could talk over the noise of the airplane engines.

"Since I was 12. I got my license at 16, the youngest age they'll let you."

"Man, I bet you have a lot of hours in the air."

"More than most people do in a car. Where exactly did you want to go?"

Bud looked down. They were now high over the can-yons, and he pulled out his little camera. Tim saw it and grinned.

"Kind of matches your earring, huh?" he teased.

"Does your wife make you do stuff like this, Tim?" Bud asked.

"Just between you and me, Bud, she made me get a tattoo. It's a heart with her name in the middle."

"I never noticed it, Tim, where is it?"

"Don't ask," Tim grinned.

Bud smiled. He started taking photos, one after another, of the redrock sea below. It was like a huge platform cut by deep canyons, all nestled beneath the Salt Mountains.

"This country is really something, isn't it?" he commented.

"Never get tired of lookin' at it," Tim replied.

"Let's angle on over to Granstaff Canyon. I want to see where that old stock trail goes down in there, if we can get down in a bit."

"Not a problem," Tim replied, angling the plane towards the huge canyon system. Bud could now make out the fins and whalebacks of Slickrock Flats above the canyon rim.

They were now down in the canyon itself, almost even with the rim, but it was wide here with plenty of room for a plane. It didn't take long for them to reach the zigzag trail that cut down into the canyon. Bud studied it carefully, looking for a large alcove, the one in his dream. He saw nothing, just the narrow trail as it went down into the depths.

"Tim, can we come up and turn around and go back in there? I need to get another look."

Tim pulled the plane up, circled out over Slickrock Flats, and Bud could see the Arrowhead poking up. There were no vehicles parked near it.

They were soon over the stock trail again, and now Bud searched the canyon walls for signs of an alcove. Nothing. It was just a dream, he reminded himself.

Now Tim was again pulling up, and they came out over Slickrock Flats again.

"Let's cruise around here a bit. I want to check the whole place out," Bud said.

They flew all over, Bud fascinated, studying places he'd hung out all his life but had never seen from the air before. Suddenly, he felt the plane angling sideways, like Tim was preparing for a barrel roll.

"Hang on to your hat," Tim grinned.

Before Bud could say a word, the plane was angled just right to clear Archy's Arch, the only arch in Slickrock Flats. Bud felt his heart go into overdrive, like his Dad's old Dodge Power Wagon when it climbed a steep hill.

They were soon through, then Tim straightened the plane back up.

Bud started laughing, partly from the adrenaline rush, partly from fear. The arch was barely wide enough for the plane, and then only at an angle. Tim grinned.

"Man, I've never flown through an arch before. That was really something. Good thing you didn't forewarn me, cause I would've been scared to death."

"Yeah, it's also slightly illegal. You won't report me to the sheriff, will you?"

Bud laughed some more. "Fly back around it so I can get some pictures."

They did, then circled back over the Arrowhead again.

"Say, Tim, you ever hear of the Slickrock Cafe?" Bud asked.

"Sure," Tim replied. "That's an old-time spot where the cowboys used to keep their horses when they were on drives. It's a natural corral high on the edge of the cliffs, but its surrounded by a natural wall of fins. And there's a big alcove in there where you can get out of the weather. The cowpunchers used to sleep in there sometimes. When the big cattle drives all kind of went by the wayside, it became a spot where locals would meet to picnic or whatever. But it's kind of lost its popularity since the BLM turned most of this into a roadless area, as it's hard to get in there now."

"You could drive in there at one time? And it's called Lost Park on the maps?"

"Yeah, there was an old road going right to it, though it's all overgrown now, what doesn't just go over the slickrock. It takes off from the old stock trail at a big pinion tree with a porcupine scar. And yes, Lost Park is what some people call it. I'll show you." With that, he turned the plane and headed back towards the Arrowhead.

They were soon nearing the edge of the canyon, but a bit further uphill from where the old stock trail went down. Huge slickrock fins edged the canyon proper. Tim dipped the plane, and there, at the canyon's edge, Bud could see where the fins formed a perfect U shape, the center carved out into a natural amphitheater, a place where one could string a rope across the entrance and have a perfect corral. Along one side of this natural park was a huge alcove tucked into a giant whaleback, a big dome, and black desert varnish draped around the alcove opening.

Bud now knew where they were. This was the spot he and Wilma Jean and Hum and Peggy Sue had come years ago in Bud's Bronco for a picnic. They'd found some Indian workings and an old campfire ring. He'd been in there lots of times with Sonny when they were kids, but they always called it Lost Park. They'd even camped out in the big alcove.

He felt a sense of relief. He'd finally found the Slickrock Cafe.

"Hey, Tim, you ever heard of the Arbuckle Cafe?" Bud asked, thinking of what Melba had said.

"Sure, it's kind of like the Slickrock Cafe. It's anywhere you brew a cup of Arbuckles coffee. Arbuckles was the first coffee that you could buy pre-roasted, back in the 1800s, and it was pretty much all the cowboys drank. Anytime they'd stop to make coffee, they were in the Arbuckle Cafe. But it looks like there's somebody down there, Bud."

Tim tilted the plane and circled back around. Sure enough, they could now see someone looking up at the plane.

"They must've been in the alcove," Bud commented.

"And what the hell is that?" Tim asked, pointing to something running around, spooked by the airplane, inside the natural corral.

"It appears to be a llama," Bud said wryly.

CHAPTER 24

Tim pulled the stick out, and the plane rose higher into the air.

"I wonder how they got in there," Bud said.

"If you look close, you can see where some ATV tracks go through the sand, right below us." Tim pointed to the faint tracks in the sand. "That would be my guess. It's a roadless area, and they must be hoping nobody notices. But what the heck is a llama doing in there?"

"I wish I knew," Bud replied. "But I have one last place I'd like you to take me—let's fly over the campground."

They were there in minutes, and Bud noticed something he didn't like—Jack's pickup was parked exactly where it had been yesterday when he and Bill had caught him trying to spy on the bikers. Bud groaned.

"See that little wash way down there?" he asked Tim. "See how low you can get to it, follow it around."

They were soon buzzing the wash, and sure enough, there was Jack, hiding, or trying to, anyway. He stood up when he saw them coming, and Bud could see he had a rifle in his hand.

"That guy's as hardheaded as a piece of granite," Bud said. "Tim, he's armed, but I don't think he would be stupid enough to shoot at us. Can you buzz him a couple of times? I don't want him in there. He's going to stir up a real hornet's nest, and I don't like things that sting."

"You bet,"Tim said, pulling the stick in. He dipped the plane so low that Bud was afraid they might crash, but he then remembered he was flying with the legendary Tim Wells.

They were so close to Jack's head that Bud thought the landing gear might hit him, but Jack quickly dropped down, then jumped up after they'd passed over, shaking his fist at them. They circled and buzzed him again, but this time, Jack was ready. He lay on the ground, pointing the rifle at them. Tim pulled the plane up.

"You sure he won't shoot?" he asked, circling back around again.

"No," Bud replied. "Maybe we'd better back off. I guess if he gets in trouble, it's his problem."

"What kind of trouble?"Tim asked.

"That's a motorcycle gang's camp, and he keeps going in there trying to run them off. He has the grazing rights here and thinks he owns the place."

"Their camp looks empty to me."

"Yeah, they're all in town right now, drinking."

"It'll be a one-man OK Corral when they get back, if he's still there,"Tim commented, pulling the stick out, the plane climbing high into the air.

• • •

They were now back at the airport, and Bud thanked Tim for the ride and wrote him a check, then headed back towards Radium, thinking that would make a nice present for Wilma Jean, to have Tim take them up sometime.

He was almost back in town, thinking about calling it a day and going home, when he got a call.

"Yell-ow."

"Bud, it's Howie. How's it going down your way?"

"Crazy as ever," Bud replied.

"Sheriff, I need your advice."

"Sure, go ahead."

"We've got a problem up here."

Good ole Howie, Bud sighed, always like pulling teeth to get anything—wisdom teeth.

"Go ahead, Howie."

"Well, as you know better than anyone, it's the end of the melon season."

"Is that a problem?" Bud asked, feeling tired and a bit exasperated.

"No, that's not it, but it's related to that. We're setting everything up in the park for Melon Days. You guys gonna get up here for it, you think? It's this weekend. They made Maureen Melon Queen."

"That's fantastic, Howie. We'd love to come, but I dunno, right now it doesn't look good. But what's the problem?"

"Well, it's the parade. Professor Krider's girls have a float, but the parade marshall won't let them in because they were late with their application."

"They need all the floats they can get. Would that just happen to be Larry Digham, Krider's main competitor?"

"You got it," Howie replied. "Any advice? I went by Krider's, and it's a darn nice float. It's a giant papier-mâché watermelon with a giant stalk and everything, on a wagon pulled by a tractor, which I'll be driving. And the girls are in the middle of the melon, peeking out and wiggling, dressed like watermelon worms."

"Like what?" Bud asked in surprise.

"Worms."

"Has Krider seen it?"

"No, he's been too busy hanging around with you, and they told me he had to go to Junction today with his wife."

"Has she seen it?"

"I don't think so. They told me it was a big surprise."

Bud was silent, not sure what to do.

"Howie, do you think that would be good advertising for Krider?"

"I dunno. Maybe not so much."

"Tell you what. You go talk to Larry, and you be sure to tell him what this float looks like. Emphasize the worms. I bet you anything he lets it in."

"Think so?" Howie asked.

"I'd bet on it," Bud replied, silently laughing to himself.

"OK, that's a big can do. Thanks, Sheriff," Howie said.

"You're welcome. And remember, bad publicity is better than no publicity."

"Roger," Howie replied.

Bud hung up the phone, wondering what Krider would think of his girls' float. Bud had a feeling the spectators would love it.

• • •

Bud drove on into town. He was tired. It had only been a few days since this whole fiasco had started, and he already longed for the peace and quiet of Krider's farm. He missed Green River—it seemed so backwater compared to Radium, and wasn't even close to being as scenic, but Bud liked its small-town feel. And sure, he was enjoying being in his old hometown again and reconnecting with old friends, but there was something about the bungalow under the big cottonwoods that he yearned for.

Maybe he was just an escapist, he thought, recalling how he'd felt the same way before he'd quit as Sheriff of Emery County.

He looked at his watch. It wasn't that late, only about 3 p.m., but it already felt like it had been a long day. He'd go home early. Lord knows he'd put in lots of overtime already, and Hans was back, so there were plenty of guys to cover for him.

Bud turned down the street to go to Peggy Sue's, hoping Wilma Jean would be there. He knew Peggy Sue would be at the hospital, as she sat with Hum during the day and the hospice nurse, Kathy, took over at night. And Wilma Jean might be there, too, sitting with Peg.

He turned to pull into the driveway, but there was no place to park. In fact, the street was lined with cars all the way up and down both sides.

He double parked behind Wilma Jean's Lincoln. As he got out and started up the sidewalk, he could make out people yelling, dogs barking, and general hooting and hollering.

Oh, no, he thought, Peggy Sue was having a party. How could she be having a party with Hum in dire straights in the hospital like that? It seemed kind of sacrilegious or something. And he sure wasn't in the mood for a party. All the action was catching up to him, he just wanted to warm up a slice of pie and go downstairs and watch TV or read.

He opened the front door. The living room was packed with people, all talking and having a great time. Hoppie and Hum's dog, Grid, were barking nonstop, and Pierre had managed to grab onto some guy's pant leg and was dragging along with him wherever he went. Wilma Jean stood in the corner, talking to a woman Bud recognized from the bowling leagues when they lived here, totally ignoring the mayhem, havoc, and barking dogs.

Oh man, this was bad, Bud thought. He wondered if he could just somehow slip downstairs, but he first had to walk through the living room and kitchen to get to the stairs that led into the basement.

He decided to go for it, pushing through the noisy crowd. All of a sudden, Pierre saw him and grabbed onto his pant leg. Hoppie was soon there also, barking madly. Bud figured it was just their way of saying welcome home, but he didn't want to deal with anything right now.

Of course Wilma Jean saw him.

"Bud! Bud! Guess what! Hum woke up!"

Bud was stunned. "Hum woke up?"

"Yeah. The doctor won't let him have company yet, but word got out and everyone just kind of congregated here. Isn't this great? Peg's down with him right now." Wilma Jean was definitely in her element—crowds of people, and Bud suspected she had helped the word get out.

"I need to get down there and talk to him," Bud told her through the din.

"It won't do any good. First, they won't let you in there, and second, it appears he can't talk yet."

"Can't talk?"

"No, the doctor says it will take time, but for now, he's not saying a word. He woke up when they put a steak dinner by his bed, ain't that a hoot? That's Hum for you."

Bud started grinning. "Hon, that's great, but I'm exhausted. I'm gonna go downstairs for a bit. We have any pie?"

"OK, I'll bring you down a piece here in a minute," Wilma Jean said.

Bud started down the stairs, Pierre dragging along, bumping down each step, while Hoppie followed along, barking his head off. Bud paused and picked up the weener dog, then continued on down the stairs, smiling.

It had turned out to be a pretty good day—Hum was awake. Bud knew they would be going back to Green River soon.

And it wasn't every day one got to fly through an arch.

CHAPTER 25

Bud had no more kicked back on the couch downstairs when his phone rang. There must be some kind of cosmic signal that went out when he relaxed, he figured, telling everyone to call him.

"Yell-ow."

"Sheriff, Cal here. I'm up at the campground, and it's about to explode. Jack Pilling's got his truck parked across the entrance so nobody can get in. That biker gang is back from drinkin', and they're pretty mad. Jack's got a rifle, and he's dancing around in the bed of the truck preaching to them, telling them they're the spawn of Satan and stuff like that. I need backup."

Bud groaned. It seemed like Jack was hell-bent on getting himself hurt.

"I thought Hans was on duty."

"He's out covering a car theft."

Bud paused. He had no idea what to do. There was no way he could get there before something happened, he knew that.

"Cal, talk some sense into him. Tell him you're gonna arrest him. Tell him you're going to go bring Melba down there, anything."

"I've already tried all that and then some."

"Look, can you get their leader, that Barry guy, on the phone?"

"I'll try. Stand by."

Soon a deep husky voice answered, "This is Barry, Spawn of Satan."

Bud grinned. At least Barry seemed to be taking it well, he didn't sound particularly mad.

"Barry, Jack Pilling's had a lot of personal problems lately. Can you guys just ignore him?"

"We could, but he's blocking us from our camp."

"I know, but look. You get your guys to come back into town and I'll buy you all a round at the Uranium. Jack will eventually get tired of sitting out there alone, and then he'll go home when he figures out he doesn't have an audience."

"That might normally work, Sheriff, but everyone's sick of 3.2 beer. Tastes like ant piss. We're tired and just want to go kick back."

Bud could hear Jack in the background. He sounded like a hellfire and brimstone preacher.

"Look Barry, Jack's no saint. He's about to go broke from gambling. He's pretty stressed."

"He gambles?" Barry broke out in deep laughter. "Our holier-than-thou preacher boy's a gambler? Look, Sheriff, don't you worry about a thing. I know just the cure for all this."

Bud grimaced. "Russian Roulette?"

"Yeah, he and I will play a few rounds. He loses, he leaves. I lose, we leave."

"Not with real ammo, though, right?"

"Right. Nobody will get hurt. If he's a gambler, he won't be able to resist the invitation."

"OK, Barry, but I'm gonna have my deputy stand by. He'll stay back, but I want him there in case anything gets out of hand. Put him on."

Bud then explained it all to Cal. He could somehow see Cal shaking his head, even though they were several miles apart.

"So, let me get this right," Cal replied. "They're going to have a big gambling party, and you're condoning it, asking me to stand by and make sure it doesn't go south?"

"Something like that, Cal. I think it might work, and everything will be OK."

"OK, Bud, but it's the first time this officer officially guarded a gambling party. I'll keep you posted."

"Roger."

• • •

Bud woke, disoriented, thinking he was home in Green River, but something wasn't right. It was dark, and he reached for the light by the bed, but it wasn't there. There was a narrow little window up high where it shouldn't be— he could make out a street light through it.

He turned over, reaching for Wilma Jean, and promptly rolled off the couch. Pierre was waiting and grabbed his pant leg, shaking it and growling.

Bud groped his way back onto the couch, finally re-membering where he was—in Hum's basement. He made his way over to a floor lamp, turning it on.

It was eerily quiet upstairs. Where was everyone?

He felt his way up the stairs and into the kitchen, turn-ing on lights as he went.

There was a note taped to the refrigerator.

"Hon, with Peg at the new Chinese rest., will bring you dinner. Fed the dogs. XXOO"

Bud looked at it awhile, wondering how long they'd been gone. He also wondered if the word "fed" should be "feed." Hoppie and Pierre sat at his feet, wagging their tails slowly, like they hadn't eaten for months and had no energy. And now Grid Bias joined them.

Bud opened the fridge, looking inside. He found some cold macaroni and cheese and divided it up into their three dog bowls. While they were eating, he looked inside some more.

Not much in there, he noted, opening the freezer. Inside was a nice pepperoni pizza, but he wasn't sure if that was a good idea. He'd probably have it cooked just about the time they brought his dinner.

He closed the door, remembering the conversation he'd had with Cal just before he'd gone to sleep. Cal hadn't called him back, and he was wondering how things were going—it had been a couple of hours. He stumbled back downstairs, found his phone, and dialed Cal.

"Deputy Murphy."

"Cal, it's Bud. How're things going?"

"I'm still up here, Sheriff. Jack seems to have won every penny these guys have, and now he's going around hugging everyone."

"Are they taking it OK? Not mad?"

"Every time he wins he dances around and tells them it's cause they're the devil's minions. But they all just laugh. He's even passing around his chew. But now that he's wiped them all out, he's leaving. He's getting into his truck right now. He told them they could stay, even though he won."

"Man, I would never have predicted this," Bud said. "Well, OK, when he leaves, you go on back into town."

"Roger. These bikers may be the spawn of Satan, but they seem to be pretty good natured."

Bud laughed. "Thanks for taking care of things, Cal. See you tomorrow."

Bud hung up just as Wilma Jean and Peggy Sue walked in the door upstairs, laughing. He was up the stairs so fast that even Pierre couldn't keep up with him.

CHAPTER 26

Bud sat in his office, feet up on his desk, showing Krider the photos he'd taken yesterday from the airplane. Krider was thinking he might have to get Tim to take him up sometime, as it seemed like the perfect way to see the country.

Bud got up and poured himself a cup of coffee from the small electric pot sitting on his windowsill. The pair had just returned from the shooting range, Bud deciding it was time that Krider learned how to use his Glock.

"Help yourself to the coffee. You see your girls' float yet?" Bud asked.

"Thanks, but I just had a cup," Krider replied. "No, it's a secret. It's in the barn, and they put a lock on the door. They won't let us see it until the parade," Krider laughed.

Bud grinned. He and Wilma Jean might have to go on up there for the parade, just to see the float, as well as Krider's reaction when he saw worms in his watermelon.

Krider had driven Bud's FJ back down from Green River, ready for more detective work. He had started the plot for a new book, based on the events of the past few days, and he was anxious to get out there and get more grist.

About then, Sandy, the dispatcher, knocked on Bud's door.

"Come in."

"Morning, fellas. Sheriff, this came on the fax this morning. Looks pretty unusual, whatever it is." She smiled, handing Bud a sheet of paper, then left.

Bud studied it for a minute, then let out a low whistle.

"Take a look." He handed Krider the paper.

"Interesting," Krider commented. "The finger bone you found appears to be about 600 years old, according to the carbon dating. That makes it Native American, probably Ute, as the Anazasi and Fremont were gone by then, and that's about when the Utes came in, around 1500. It's stained with malachite, a mineral formed from the weathering of copper ore, which means it came from some kind of copper-bearing formation. The lab's referring it to the local BLM archaeologist for follow-up, as this is their jurisdiction."

"You can bet that whoever dug it up is in for a world of hurt, as grave-digging isn't too popular in these parts—highly illegal," Bud commented.

"It could've washed out, eroded," Krider replied.

"True," Bud answered, "but the nearest place with copper is a good 20 miles from Slickrock Flats—the Little Indian mine up on the flanks of the Salts—or Copper Ridge in the other direction, over by the national park. Either way, it didn't come from Slickrock. That's all Navajo Formation, and there's no copper in Navajo sandstone."

"Maybe a raven brought it there," Krider offered.

"I think a raven brought it, but not any distance. It would've dropped it before it got that far," Bud replied.

Sandy tapped on the door, then stuck her head in.

"Another fax, Sheriff. You're keeping the lab busy."

Bud took the paper, pursing his lips and twiddling his ear-post while studying it.

"Look at this," he said grimly, handing the paper to Krider.

"Too bad," Krider replied quietly after reading it. "The bullet came from Jack's rifle. But how can they tell?"

Bud answered, "Every gun has imperfections in its barrel. If you have both the gun and the bullet, they can look through a microscope and see if the striations in the barrel match those on the bullet. The bullet picks up these patterns as it moves through the barrel."

"Interesting. Now what?" Krider asked.

"I'm not sure. We could go arrest him, but I think there's more here than meets the eye. If we arrest Jack now, it might jeopardize the rest of the investigation. I dunno. I know that finger bone came from one of the Malachites. And I know Jack well enough to know he's no grave digger. I think we have more than one culprit here, Prof, and I want them all brought to justice. And we don't know yet who was after Hum."

"Maybe it was Jack. Maybe Hum saw him shoot Jimmy."

"No, I think Hum would've said something, and why not just kill Hum if he'd witnessed the murder? I think the thought of going to prison would've been a good enough incentive for Jack to shoot."

"True," Krider said. "But now what?" He was glad he'd been practicing with his Glock and felt fairly comfortable with it, but he sure wasn't up to shooting anyone.

"Hang on a minute, I need to make a call," Bud said, dialing the Blue Jay Pit.

After talking for a few minutes, he hung up the phone, then turned to Krider.

"Charlie says Jimmy Ottin bought the largest shipment he's ever sold, three weeks ago—150 pounds of the stuff."

"Wow," Krider said. "Could he sell that much in his shop?"

"I was just in there, and Sonny has maybe 30 pounds on display. I would guess he could sell that amount in six months or a year. But 150 pounds? Probably in a few years."

"Maybe he was anticipating a malachite shortage and playing the market."

"I don't know," Bud answered. "The Blue Jay Pit has a long ways to go before it plays out, I would think. My guess is it has something to do with the Malachites. And something says it's time to pay a visit to the Slickrock Cafe."

CHAPTER 27

Bud parked his FJ by the Arrowhead, and he and Krider got out and started down the old stock trail. They were both wearing jackets, as it looked like the weather was turning, and it might rain, or worse yet, bring an early autumn snow.

"You pretty sure you can find the place?" Krider asked.

"Yeah," Bud replied, "I went up there dozens of times when I was a kid, and a few times since then, too. It's easy to find, you just turn west at the Porky Tree, that old pinion with the scar. I knew there was something familiar about it, but I just didn't make the connection. To me, it was always Lost Park."

They cautiously walked down the trail, searching the deep sand for tracks. Krider was ahead of Bud, and he stopped, pointing to the ground.

"Looks like horse tracks."

Bud stopped to examine them. "Pretty fresh, too. I wonder if Jack's down in here. He's been in and out of here some, judging from the chew we found the other day. He could easily get here on horseback from his place, in fact, I thought about going up there and borrowing a couple of horses from him to make it easier to get in here—Sonny and I used to go borrow Jack's horses and ride around, but

I changed my mind when I found out the gun and bullet matched."

"He might not want to help us find who killed Jimmy," Krider commented. "Especially since it appears to have been him."

"Right. Or someone who had his rifle. He could still be innocent," Bud replied.

"True," Krider said, "But unlikely, given his bad temper. But it wouldn't be the first time I've been surprised—heck, I'm sometimes surprised by the plots in my own books."

They were at the pinion tree in short order, where they stopped again to look for clues, hoping something new would turn up. Nothing had changed, except Jack's tracks seemed to go on down the trail, not turning towards the Cafe.

"He must be out scoping for cattle," Krider said.

"No, it's too late in the season, Prof. He's already moved them all down to the flats out north of town. I have no idea what he's doing, maybe just out riding."

"Yeah, maybe just out riding," Krider said. "Unarmed, I hope."

They now left the stock trail, following a faint trail that led to the west, parallel with Granstaff Canyon. They were soon on slickrock and could see serrated edges cut into the rock.

"This was once an old uranium exploration road," Bud commented. "They used an old D90 Cat to scrape it. If you keep an eye out, you might still see some old core samples scattered around from the drill rigs."

"I suspected as much, knowing what I do about Radium history," Krider replied. "What, in about the 1950s?"

"That and on into the 60s," Bud replied. "My dad was a uranium miner, but over in the Yellow Cat District."

After they'd gone about a half mile, Bud stopped and went behind a small outcropping of rock, motioning Krider to follow.

He said, quietly, "Prof, we've got a good half-mile or more until we get to the Cafe, but I'm starting to feel a sense of something—I won't say danger, but maybe caution would describe it. If there are still people up at the Cafe, we might not want them to know we're coming."

"They may already know, Bud, from the way that Black Beast seemed to know when we were at the tree back there every time we went there."

"Yeah, you're right."

"So where is the Black Beast, by the way. Isn't it about time for it to make an appearance?" Krider asked.

"It only comes out at dusk, Prof. You can't see it except then."

"Right, it's a cougar—or maybe a jaguar, and they're nocturnal. Maybe it came up from New Mexico. I've heard the jaguar is extending its range further and further north."

"Maybe, but I think this one's range is determined solely by how dark it is and the luminescence of its light source."

"What the heck, Bud. You've figured something out and forgot to tell me," Krider replied. "You said earlier you thought it was faked..."

Before Bud could answer, the distant hum of an ATV cut through the quiet, and it was soon near them.

Bud and Krider peeked around the rocks, watching. Bud knew it was probably the same ATV he'd seen from the air the previous day parked at the Slickrock Cafe.

Before long, the sound reverberated all around them, amplified by the rocks. Bud could now see it coming, and as it got closer, he could see that the driver was the same man he'd seen leading the llama, his face covered with a dark beard and dressed in the same red poncho, wool hat and knee pants. It was a side-by-side, and next to him sat a man who was dressed in, of all things, a dark suit, light yellow dress shirt with matching tie, and black shiny shoes, his hair perfectly groomed. He looked like he'd been dropped direct from the streets of a large city.

Krider poked Bud a bit in the ribs as they went by, then said, "Is that the Peruvian guy you saw the other night? I thought maybe you'd been hallucinating, but now I think I'm the one hallucinating."

The ATV headed in the general direction of the Slickrock Cafe.

Bud replied, "C'mon, Prof. We need to get over there and see what's going on. But let's go around the back way so nobody sees us."

Bud motioned for Krider to follow him as he stepped out of the rocks and headed for a passage between two huge fins.

"I hope we don't get lost back in here," Krider replied a bit nervously.

"It's OK, I know this place like the back of my hand. And I have a photographic memory for places, Prof, I never forget routes. I can follow them in my mind as if I were right there."

They were soon in the narrow passage, pushing through stands of wavy-leafed Gambel's oak and single-leaf ash that flourished in the shady shelter. It made the going hard, but they emerged from the other end, following a wash that also emerged.

"We need to make better time than this," Bud said, "Or we'll miss the action."

They now began climbing a smaller fin.

"I thought this stuff was slick," Krider commented.

"It's slicker than ice when it's wet," Bud said. "See all that tiny greenish lichen growing on the north side here? When it's wet, this stuff is like an ice-skating rink."

Krider looked up. "We may get a chance to test it out." He pointed to thick black clouds that seemed to be collecting right over them.

"Damn," Bud replied.

They now continued along a series of smaller domes, climbing to the crest of each, then back down, making their way in the general direction of the Slickrock Cafe. Soon they were at the edge of Granstaff Canyon.

"Now what?" asked Krider.

"OK, now we have to be really quiet, because the Cafe is just on the other side of these big fins. We're going to climb out there where we can see down into the Cafe and hopefully not be seen."

Bud pointed to a narrow fin that dropped dramatically into the edge of the canyon. One side was eroded off, and the other side angled into what appeared to be a giant bowl.

"Watch your step. Once we get on top, there's a shallow basin we can hide in, it has a couple of small junipers in it."

"Jeez," Krider replied. "That's a bit heady. I'm not too good with heights, Bud."

"OK, no problem. You just stay put here and wait. I don't want you doing anything you're not comfortable with."

"I'm going to climb up over there and scout around," Krider answered, pointing to another wider fin behind them."

"OK, but be careful. There's someone else out here with a good vantage point, and they might see you, so try to stay hidden."

"Someone else?" Krider asked, but Bud didn't hear him. He was gone, crawling up the steep and exposed edge of the big slickrock fin.

• • •

Bud was soon on top, where he inched into the small basin and hid behind a thick juniper tree. He was at the perfect angle to see down into the Slickrock Cafe, and he could see the ATV parked at the opening of the natural corral, which had been roped off.

The llama he'd seen earlier was still there, and it stood quietly looking into a giant alcove on the wall opposite Bud. The alcove was too deep for Bud to see into it, but he knew the two men were in there, from the way the llama's ears were perked.

Bud nestled down deeper in the small basin, hoping the animal wouldn't see him or sense he was there. He didn't want to alarm it and give himself away.

He waited for some time, nothing happening, but suddenly he saw the llama startle and run to the opposite side of the corral. He could now hear what appeared to be chanting, and it was coming from the alcove. Now a pale blue light appeared deep in the interior, and a chill went up Bud's spine.

This was just like in his dream, he thought. The Malachites were in there, and so were the two men. Bud wasn't superstitious, but he couldn't help but wonder if something from another world hadn't somehow made its way in there, something with a supernatural strangeness. He fought the urge to flee.

He pulled back a bit, trying to get a grip on himself. He sat there, breathing deep, thinking back to the time he and his dad were walking through a deep forest up in the Salts one black night, late at getting back to camp, when something white came bobbing down the trail towards them. Bud was just a child, and he'd been scared to death. His dad silently pulled him off to the side of the trail, and the white bobbing thing passed on by.

Bud had tearfully asked his dad what it was, and his dad had told him it was a horse—a dark horse with a white blaze. The horse's head moved up and down as it walked, making the blaze appear to bob. His dad had then told him that there was a rational explanation for everything, no matter how strange it might seem.

Bud now pushed his way back to where he could see again, more relaxed and steady. The light was flashing around in the alcove, and he could hear a loud moaning. Now, two men came out and stood there for a bit, just in time for a loud scream to pierce the air.

It was the Black Beast, and from his vantage point, Bud could see it coming towards the alcove at a remarkable speed. The two men ran for the ATV, jumping on it and starting it up, quickly turning and fleeing, barely opening and closing the rope gate, just as the Black Beast came from the rocks and followed them, still screaming.

Bud was now grinning. It was exactly as he thought. The Black Beast had suddenly disappeared into thin air the moment the two men had fled. It was a projection—a good one, and whoever was doing it had a powerful light source and a good rendition of a jaguar, as well as a really good sound system. And it was coming from a fin somewhere over behind him. He couldn't quite make out the source, as it was up higher and more distant.

He stood and carefully started back down, looking for Krider. The clouds were now closing in. He thought of Jack Pilling and wondered where he was and if he were involved in any of this.

Bud was now back down off the fin, and he saw neither hide nor hair of Krider. He wished he'd paid closer attention to where Krider had said he was going, something about climbing a fin to look out. He wanted to yell out for him, but he knew that whoever was running the projection light had to be nearby.

He tried tracking him, but the slickrock yielded no clues.

CHAPTER 28

Bud now heard the sound of hoofbeats coming. Someone was riding across the slickrock at a fast pace, and they were coming straight towards him.

He pulled out his Ruger and crouched down behind some nearby rocks, peeking out just in time to see a rider on a paint horse coming at a fast gallop. Dangerous thing to do, Bud thought, given that slickrock didn't provide much grip for a horse's hooves, and a light misty rain had started.

He couldn't make out who the rider was, but he held his gun, ready to shoot if necessary. As the horse got closer, he recognized the animal—it was Patches, Jack's cowpony. He looked closer—yes, it was Jack, and he was riding recklessly fast.

Just as it got to the rocks where Bud hid, the horse turned sharply, nearly lost its footing, then went on, down towards the Porky Tree.

Soon horse and rider were gone.

"What the hell was that about?" Bill said out loud to himself. "He sure was in a hurry."

The rain was starting to come down now, and Bud didn't know what to do. Where the heck was Krider? Bud pulled out his cell phone, but no signal. There were only a few hours of daylight left, and Krider could wander for days in this wilderness of fins and never have a clue where he was. Bud recalled the many search and rescue missions he'd been a part of when he lived here, some not so successful.

He started up a big fin, the one he thought Krider had said he was going to climb. It was now getting slick, and Bud could feel his feet sliding backwards a bit for every step forward. This was a cold rain, and hypothermia was a real factor when one was out like this. He pulled his hood closer around his face to keep the dripping water out.

He was now on top of the fin, and he tried to scope all around, but misty gray clouds blocked his view—except he could now see down towards the pinion tree, and something looked odd.

He pulled his little pocket binoculars out and tried to make out what he was seeing. Sure enough, there was a horse standing there by the trail. Something dark was nearby, and the horse appeared to have its head down, looking at it. It looked like a body.

"Oh, no," Bud said, "It's Jack." He carefully but quickly descended the fin, then began half-jogging in the direction of the tree. He was soon off the slickrock into a jumble of rocks and junipers.

He was quickly at the tree and grabbed Patches's reins, which were trailing along the ground. The horse knew him and didn't try to get away.

Sure enough, Jack lay at Patches's feet, out cold. Patches's left side was covered with wet sand, and Bud knew the horse had lost its balance and fallen, knocking Jack out cold.

"Not another head injury," Bud said to himself, carefully looking at Jack's head, trying to see if there was a wound. He soon found a long gash. It appeared Jack had managed to hit a tree limb on his way down.

Bud then ripped a strip off his own shirttail, wrapping it around Jack's head to stop the bleeding, but the rag was soon soaked. He started to feel a sense of helplessness. Jack needed help, and pronto, and Bud really couldn't do much for him. He pulled out his cell phone to call for help, but there was still no service. The big fins were blocking the tower, which was way up on the Salts.

Bud didn't know what to do. His first-aid training told him to apply pressure, but the wound was too large. He tried to tighten the makeshift shirt bandage, but it didn't seem to slow down the bleeding any. He worried about Jack going into shock.

After what seemed to him like forever, Bud made a decision. He quickly got onto Patches and took off up the old stock trail. He had to go for help. It was Jack's only chance.

• • •

Bud quickly made it to the Arrowhead, where he now had cell service, and dialed 911, explaining the situation to Sandy, wondering if they could get here fast enough. What Jack really needed was a Flight for Life helicopter, but the weather would never permit a landing. It was too risky.

Bud was getting ready to go back to Jack when he heard the sound of someone coming down the road.

It at first sounded like an ATV, then a dirt bike, then a full-on street motorcycle, maybe several. Finally, he saw the source—it was Barry and Jeff. They pulled up close to him, but when they noticed Bud was having a hard time holding Patches back, they cut their engines.

"Nice day, isn't it, Sheriff?" Barry grinned. "You always go riding in the rain?"

"Yup, just like you do," Bud replied. "Barry, Jack's back in there, his horse threw him and he's bleeding bad and getting cold. I called 911, but I'm worried they won't get here in time. I'm going back down to him—could you guys stay and tell them to turn here and go down about a quarter mile when they arrive?"

With that, Bud turned Patches, nudged him into a gallop, and went back down the sandy trail to where Jack lay, still bleeding.

● ● ●

Bud jumped off Patches, tying him to the big tree. He then tore off another bit of his shirt and wadded it into a bandage, holding it over the wound, again trying to slow down the bleeding. This seemed to help a little, but Jack needed real medical help. The rain was now turning into a light snow. He needed to somehow get Jack warm.

He paused, almost stopping breathing so he could hear better. He thought he could hear a sound—someone was coming! There was no way the EMT guys from Radium could be here that fast, Bud thought. He cringed, wondering if it was the two guys he'd seen at the Slickrock Cafe coming back.

But things didn't sound right, it wasn't an ATV. In fact, it wasn't any sound Bud had ever heard down in the slickrock before—it sounded like a motorcycle.

How could anyone get a motorcycle in here? Bud wondered. The air currents from the canyons must be playing tricks on him. But he turned just as a BMW motorcycle made its way through the sand, occasionally spinning out, and then came right up to where he and Jack were and stopped.

It was Barry.

Barry jumped off the bike and ran and crouched next to Jack. He then ran back to his bike, grabbed something from the panniers, then was back. He had a medical kit, and was soon checking Jack over, feeling his pulse and looking at his gums to see if he were in shock. He took the makeshift bandage off Jack's head and inspected the wound, then quickly applied a pressure bandage from his kit, stopping the bleeding.

Bud just stood there, watching, then finally came to his senses.

"Is there anything I can do? Are you an EMT?" Bud asked Barry.

"He's in shock. Get that IV out of my panniers and help me get it on him. Is there any way you could build a fire next to him? And no, I'm not an EMT, I'm a doctor."

Bud couldn't believe it—Barry, the head of the Minot Marauders, AKA the Devil's Minions and Spawn of Satan, was a medical doctor. And he was going to save Jack's life, Bud just knew it, right here and now.

Bud felt like he himself might go into shock at the irony of it all.

CHAPTER 29

Bud had built a fire, and the falling snowflakes sizzled as they fell into it, transforming back into water. He and Barry stood nearby, trying to warm up. The EMTs had arrived and were carrying Jack back up the trail on a stretcher to get him to the waiting ambulance and the hospital, where he'd get stitches, probably spend a few days, then go home.

"Better get going if you don't want that bike stuck in here," Bud advised. "You guys are gonna freeze camping tonight."

"We're going into town, kind of a treat, spend the night in a condo. But we're leaving our tents up, as we may spend a couple more nights if the weather gets better."

"What then?" Bud asked.

"Then it's back to work, but we're first going to spend a couple of days up in Green River. I've heard Melon Days is a lot of fun."

Now Bud thought of Krider, somewhere out in the slick-rock. "I gotta get going myself," he said. "You're a doctor, but what do the other guys do?"

"Well, Jeff owns a dairy, but about everyone else is a professional of some kind—one's a banker, another's an accountant, that kind of thing. We do a trip like this every year."

Bud grinned. He recalled when they'd passed him going into Radium and he'd suspected as much. He then recalled Krider telling him they weren't career bikers, how Jack said they were doctors and lawyers—and then Howie telling him how dangerous they all were.

Bud got up and kicked sand into the sizzling fire.

"I got a guy out here who appears to be lost, and I gotta go find him before dark. He's not prepared to spend the night out in the snow." Bud went over and untied Patches.

Barry looked concerned. "Somebody lost? Man, you keep busy, don't you?"

"Not usually this busy, Barry. I'm pretty worried about this guy. He's the one who was with me when we found the snake."

"Bill Krider? Oh man, he didn't strike me as a hard-core outdoorsman. What's he doing lost?" Barry's voice trailed off as he went to his motorcycle, got something out, then came back.

"I wish I knew," Bud replied.

"Take this," Barry offered, holding up gloves, a wool hat, and several granola bars.

Bud stuffed it all into his jacket pockets. "Thanks. Would you call my office and tell them to call Jack's wife and tell her what happened? Just dial 911, Sandy will pick up. And Barry, thanks for everything. Now you get outta here while you can."

With that, Bud swung his leg over the saddle, and he and Patches turned and headed down the trail, disappearing into the swirling snow.

• • •

Bud knew he had only an hour at the most before it was dark, but he had to try to find Krider. He was responsible for him being lost, he knew better than to let him go his own way alone, especially out here. Krider just wasn't the seasoned outdoorsman Bud was, and even the best had been lost out on the slickrock. It was easy to get disoriented in the fins and whalebacks.

Patches was a good horse, and Bud knew he could cover a lot more ground on him than he could walking. It had kind of been a godsend for him that Jack had fallen, but then, not so much for Jack. But otherwise Bud would be out here on foot, and he knew it was impossible to cover much territory that way. He wondered again why Jack had been in such a hurry.

Bud put on the hat and gloves Barry gave him, grateful for them. He wondered why he hadn't checked the weather a little more closely before he and Krider ventured out on this escapade. Neither of them had come prepared. He knew better. These early autumn storms weren't that uncommon.

He was quickly back to where he'd last seen Krider, at the base of the big fin, but nothing was different, no prof. He now was beginning to feel desperate. To hell with whoever might be out here, he was going to start yelling.

He began yelling Krider's name, then listened, but heard nothing but the rustle of the dead leaves of a nearby single-leaf ash as the breeze picked up. He then rode a bit further into the fins and called again. Nothing.

Bud rode around like this for over an hour, back and forth, crisscrossing between fins and yelling, with no results, and he finally decided to angle back over to the Slickrock Cafe. The light was now diffuse, and he could tell the sun was setting, even through the thick cloud cover. The air was colder, and he was beginning to feel wet and chilled, which was a bad sign. Patches was now soaked. He couldn't stay out here much longer, and he was now wondering why he hadn't told Barry to call Cal and get a search team going. It would soon be too dark.

He was now back where he'd first seen Jack riding like a bat out of hell. He began yelling again.

Wait—over there—what was that? He stopped and strained to hear, but now a cold breeze was picking up. Must've been the wind, moaning through the junipers, he thought.

He yelled again, but this time he was sure he heard a voice. A chill went down his back. It was distant, but it seemed to be saying, "Bud! Bud!"

He slowly turned Patches and headed towards the sound, his hat now off so he could hear better.

"Bud! Bud!"

There was no question about it, he'd heard his name. And it seemed to be coming from the direction of the Slick-rock Cafe. Carefully, oh so carefully now, he walked Patches towards the corral opening. The rope was untied, and the llama was gone. Someone had come back for it while they were tending to Jack. Snow now covered the junipers in the corral, making them look like white specters.

Bud rode Patches on into the corral, then dismounted and tied the rope, closing the gate. No way was he going to lose Patches, and this would ensure he didn't take off.

There was no place to tie Patches except to a juniper, and there were too many branches to deal with, so Bud tied the reins to the saddle horn. Patches stood silently in the snow, watching Bud. He knew the horse just wanted to be home, in the barn, warm and dry and eating hay. He could relate.

Bud now walked towards the alcove. The sun was rapidly fading, and Bud felt that sense he sometimes felt when out in the backcountry in the twilight, a longing for comfort and light. He called out again, "Bill! Bill!"

Now he heard his name again. The maw of the alcove went deep into the cliff with a blackness his eyes couldn't penetrate. He hesitated, but again he heard what sounded like Krider calling his name. Krider was in the alcove.

Bud drew his gun.

Bud's instincts said not to go, but his empathy overrode them. He had to help Krider. He started into the alcove, his gun in his hand, then stopped.

He slowly backed out, then leaned against the wall of the big fin, next to the alcove's opening. He was having a flashback, he thought. This was exactly like his dream. So exactly that it couldn't be real. He must be dreaming again. He stood there for a moment, snowflakes falling onto his face.

He now sidled into the thick blackness. This time, no one was going to grab him, there would be no icy cold bony fingers. He wasn't dreaming, and this was the real deal. If anyone grabbed his neck, it would be someone alive, and he wasn't going to let that happen.

He continued on, placing his feet with care, trying to see through the inky blackness. He was now deep in the alcove, but there was no blue glowing light, and his hands weren't turning into green stone.

He heard something rustle.

He said, quietly, "Prof?"

"Thank God it's you, Bud," Krider's voice said through the darkness. "I was thinking you were somebody else and was wondering if I might have to shoot."

"I was thinking the same thing," Bud said. He pulled out his cell phone and dimly lit the alcove with its display.

Krider stood over in the corner, looking wet and cold and bedraggled. Above him, carved into the wall, was a giant Incan cougar, and next to that was a snake. They appeared to be the work of the same artist as up above the Porky Tree.

Bud turned, shining the light around the big alcove. Not far from Krider was a dark shadow, but Bud couldn't make out what it was.

He walked over closer. Now he could see what appeared to be a dark-green throne made of heavy cardboard, and on it sat two skeletons, one with the tip of its little finger missing. They stared at him with empty eye sockets, and Bud could see that both skeletons were encrusted with beautiful green stones.

It was the Malachites.

CHAPTER 30

"Wow, so those must be the Malachites," Krider said. "Too weird. Bud, somebody's coming."

"We need to get out of here now," Bud replied.

They ran to the opening of the alcove, and Bud caught Patches, untying the reins, then swinging up into the saddle.

Krider undid the gate, and Bud rode through, then stopped, motioning for Krider to get on behind him. Krider put his foot into the stirrup and tried to climb behind Bud, kicking Patches in the flanks. The horse sidestepped a bit, then waited until Krider was up behind Bud, holding on tightly.

"Keep your feet up away from him and don't kick," Bud said. "And hang on."

The trail was now almost pitch black, but the falling snow helped define its edges. They could hear an ATV coming towards them. Bud deftly reined Patches off the trail behind the Porky Tree, just as two ATVs drove by.

Driving one was Cal, and Hans the other. Behind Hans was Barry.

Bud and Krider both started yelling at the same time. The ATVs stopped.

"You boys know this is a roadless area?" Bud asked, grinning.

Krider slipped off Patches and stumbled towards the ATVs. He had started shivering, and Barry was soon checking him over.

"He's going hypothermic, Bud. We need to get him someplace warm."

Krider climbed onto the ATV behind Cal.

"Take him into town ASAP," Bud said. "I'm going to take Patches on up to Jack's place. Cal, could you send someone to pick me up?"

"Aren't you cold?" Hans asked.

"I am," Bud answered. "But I'll be OK."

"Bud, you need to come with us. We can take Patches into town for the night. We can put him in with the Game and Fish horses," Cal said.

"No, Cal, I want to take him home. Patches has done a lot today, and he deserves his own warm barn. And we'll just have to take him home tomorrow if we don't tonight."

"Don't be hardheaded, Bud. Let's take him into town, it's closer. It's snowing, and you have to be getting hypothermic. That way I can follow you. I got that darn ATV trailer on back."

Hans interrupted, "Cal, the Sheriff has the constitutional right to go wherever he wants."

Bud laughed, touched Patches' sides with his heels, and was soon gone, trotting through the snow up the sandy trail towards the Arrowhead.

• • •

Bud was now back at Hum and Peg's house, having taken the horse back to Jack's and settling it down into the warm barn with several flakes of good alfalfa hay and a bucket of water. The lights were off in the house and Melba's car was gone, and Bud figured she was at the hospital with Jack. Cal had shown up and given him a ride home.

Bud kicked back on the couch, dry clothes on, boots off, and feet pointed in the direction of the gas-log fireplace. Krider sat next to it in an easy chair, wrapped in a wool blanket and drinking hot tea.

"Man, that was quite the adventure," Krider said. "I can't wait to get home and write about it."

"Your wife should be here soon," Bud replied. "I'm just glad it turned out for the best."

"Me, too," Krider replied. "But I forgot to tell you what I found. My lips were too numb to talk."

Bud laughed. "Yeah, but fortunately not too cold to yell when the guys came by on the ATVs. But what was it?"

"It was on top of a fin, but one where you could get in there with an ATV, not that steep. I was up there looking around, and I saw what I thought was a rock. I went over to sit on it and take a break, but it turned out to be a tarp."

"Way out there in the fins?"

"Yeah, and under it was a big generator—attached to sound and lighting equipment. It took a minute, but I finally figured out that it had to be the heart and soul of the Black Beast."

Bud sat up. "Well, I'll be go to. Just as I suspected. That's why the scream sounded kind of mechanical."

"Yeah, and there was a cutout of a cougar there, nicely done, and binoculars. And Bud..."

"Yeah?"

"The generator had something written on it—'Property of Red River by Night.'"

"I thought so," Bud answered. "Nice work, Prof." He paused. "It sounds like your wife's here." They could hear the dogs barking upstairs and Wilma Jean laughing.

"One last thing, Bud," Krider continued. "Remember those huge cougar tracks we found? There was a track just like it up there."

"No way!" Bud replied.

"Yeah, and it was on the end of a stick. Carved out of wood."

"No kidding. They were planting tracks to make the Black Beast seem more real. But why?"

"I don't know, Bud," Krider said solemnly, standing to go. He then extended his hand to Bud.

Bud stood, shaking it warmly.

"Prof, take care, get warmed up, and thanks again for everything. You make a helluva good partner."

"Likewise," Krider replied. "I'll be back."

• • •

Bud kicked back again, his feet now finally starting to tingle a bit.

He thought back. It had been a busy day, and he'd finally discovered the Malachites. They were indeed real, not a dream.

But he was still no closer to figuring out who had killed Jimmy Ottin, unless it had been Jack Pilling. For some reason, Bud didn't think so, but he just wasn't sure.

He had one more person he needed to talk to before he called it a day. He'd promised Wilma Jean he would take her out for dinner, but he knew she would understand if he were a bit late.

• • •

Bud walked down the hospital hall, peeking his head in when he got to Hum's room. Hum was eating what looked like a big steak dinner, while Peggy Sue helped him, cutting it up and putting steak sauce on it.

"Has he said anything yet?" Bud asked quietly, nodding towards Hum.

"Well, I think he said 'milk' when he wanted a glass of milk with his dinner. But he at least seems to be feeling OK."

"You get better fast," Bud told Hum. "I'm still working on finding whoever it was that conked you on the head."

Hum seemed to be nodding his head a bit, and acted for a minute like he wanted to say something.

Bud continued, "I gotta go next door. There's a new patient in there as of this afternoon I need to talk to."

Bud walked to the next room, then looked up and down the hall. There was no nurse in sight, so he went on in and sat down by the figure in the bed.

"Evening, Jack, you doin' OK?" Bud asked.

The figure mumbled something about wanting a drink, so Bud helped him sit partway up, then handed him the glass of water on the stand next to his bed. Jack moaned a bit, took a few sips, then crumpled back onto the bed.

"Bet that hurts, don't it? Why you'd wanna go and tangle with a tree like that I wouldn't know."

Jack moaned a bit more, then Bud thought he heard him say, "Patches."

"I took Patches up to your barn and fed and watered him, Jack, he's fine," Bud answered. "Why the heck were you riding so damn fast, anyway?"

Bud now definitely heard Jack say something about a black cougar.

So that was it, Jack had seen the Black Beast and was scared to death. Bud bet Patches hadn't even noticed. He should've trusted his horse, Bud mused.

"Your pillow OK there, Jack? You need a nurse? Why were you out riding around in such bad weather, anyway?"

Jack mumbled something about Sonny Ottin, something about him running llamas up there when he shouldn't. Bud continued, even though he knew Jack was hurting. But he also knew it might be the only time he could really corner the man, especially if they released him from the hospital soon—corner him without arresting him first, anyway.

"Melba knows you're here, she's probably already been in here, I would guess. But Jack, I know this is a bad time to bring it up, but are you and Sonny involved in some kind of gambling deal?"

"No," Jack said.

"OK, I hope not. But Jack, what are you running from in your past? And why were you guys following me clear up to Green River? And why'd you wanna go and kill Jimmy Ottin?"

Jack now pulled himself up onto his elbows, groaning.

He whispered, "Dammit, Bud, I'm hurting, you can see that. I never killed Jimmy, I swear."

"The lab says the gun and bullet match, Jack."

"They match? Can't argue with that. Alright, you're right, you caught your murderer, I killed him." He slipped back onto the pillow.

With that, Jack turned his head, and Bud knew he wouldn't get another word out of the man, at least not that night. But he couldn't resist adding one more tidbit.

"Jack, you remember Barry? The leader of the Minot Marauders, or what you call the Devil's Minions? He's a doctor, Jack, and he saved your life. I wouldn't be surprised if he doesn't come in to visit you soon. Well, see you around, you get better."

With that, Bud stepped out of the room, went home where Wilma Jean waited, then took her out to Smitty's Steak House for a late dinner, chewing on the feeling he had that Jack was lying.

CHAPTER 31

Bud was tired. He swore his feet were still cold from yesterday's shenanigans. He woke up wanting badly to take the day off, but he'd come into the office instead. Maybe he'd quit early, but right now he needed to make a call. He opened the phone book, then dialed a number.

"Red River by Night, can I help you?"

"This is Bud Shumway, Interim Sheriff here in Radium. Would it be possible to speak to a manager?"

"Speaking."

"Sorry, I didn't get your name."

"Mary Ketchum. I'm the owner."

"Oh, that's great, Mary. I took my niece on your boat tour once, and we sure enjoyed it. But I'm wondering if you rent out equipment, you know, sound or light stuff?"

"Well, no, we don't," Mary replied.

"You don't. Well, are you missing anything?"

"Not that I'm aware of. Did you find something of ours?"

Bud ignored her question. "Do you know a kid named Tommy Ottin?"

"Sure, Tommy worked here for a bit, but we had to let him go."

"Mind if I ask why?"

"He was a seasonal and the season ended."

"Would you hire him again?"

"Oh, sure, he's a good kid, a hard worker. He gets a little sullen once in awhile—moody might be a better word, but I overlooked it because he works so hard."

"OK, Mary, well that's all I need to know. Appreciate your time."

"You're welcome. Bring your niece back down and we'll give you a 20% locals' discount."

"Now there's an idea. We'll have to do that. You have a nice day."

"Oh wait—Sheriff? I forgot, but we do have some equipment that hasn't been returned, and it's a bit overdue. Jimmy Ottin came in a few weeks ago and borrowed some stuff. He's helped out my business a lot by steering people my way, so I let him take it, but it would be nice to get it back, if you see him."

"Well, I won't be seeing him, unless something unusual happens, but I'll put the word out."

"Thanks very much."

• • •

Well, that was interesting, Bud thought, fiddling with his ear-post. At least the equipment wasn't stolen, which had been his first guess.

He now figured he knew who had taken it up on the fin—and that same person had to have been involved with the Malachites. But who was carrying on his legacy, now that Jimmy was gone? Someone sure was.

Bud had a pretty strong hunch that someone was Sonny, and maybe even Tommy. Kind of a family deal, which was how the Ottins had always been. They ran the shop together, rock hounded together, broke the law together. But why carry on without Jimmy?

Whatever was going on, Bud figured it probably involved money. Maybe it was wrapped up with a gambling ring run by Sonny, or maybe Jack was involved—he liked to gamble. But it was becoming clear that it involved a good deal of drama, and Bud had no idea why. And it appeared the Black Beast was conjured up to scare people away when anyone got too close to whatever was going on.

Someone had decided the Slickrock Cafe would be a good place for some mysterious Peruvian theatrics. And why the skeletons? Where did they come from? Bud knew they were 600 years old, but who had found them? And green bones? They were the real deal, they hadn't been dyed—the report had said it was a malachite stain. And who was the dark-bearded fellow in the Peruvian dress leading a llama? Where did he fit in? And the city guy in the suit on the ATV with him?

Bud paused. That fellow with the llama was the same size as Sonny Ottin, now that he thought of it. And why was Sonny taking money there in the cafe and looking so suspicious?

Then again, maybe it didn't involve money, but was some kind of religious cult or something, with the stylized petroglyphs and symbols, something that revolved around the Malachites. After all, they'd been on a sort of throne, like deities. Jack seemed to have the devil on the brain, calling everyone the devil's minions and preaching to them— was he involved? Bud thought Jack would make a good preacher—he had the fiery temperament—but he'd have to give up gambling and chew. But if Jack had been in on it, why would he be afraid of the Black Beast? He would've known it was fake.

Bud now got up and poured himself a cup of coffee from his little electric pot, then sat back down, his feet up on his desk, thinking about everything that had happened in the past week or so, fiddling with his ear-post. He noted that it no longer itched.

How in hellsbells did he end up as Interim Sheriff, and why had he agreed to take on the job? There were guys here who could've done it—Cal for example—and done a fine job, too. Shoots, Cal would probably have figured everything out by now and had the culprit in jail, which would probably mean arresting Jack Pilling.

Bud thought about his last few months as a melon farmer and how nice and peaceful they'd been. What was he thinking, coming back down here? Sure, it had been kind of nice reconnecting with old friends and all, but he didn't need to be sheriff to do that. It was only about 50 miles from Green River on down here, he and Wilma Jean could come anytime they wanted, and it would be a lot less stressful.

He was missing the bungalow again and all it represented, his secure and cozy life with Wilma Jean and the kids, Pierre and Hoppie.

It looked like Hum was going to eventually be OK, and Bud could go back to melon farming, but he was now worried that Wilma Jean might want to stay in Radium. She had been successful here before and could do it again. She could sell the bowling alley and cafe in Green River, and that would give her the capital she needed to start over here.

Bud was sure Hum would give him a job as a deputy, maybe even as undersheriff, but he wasn't so sure he wanted it. He just wanted things to be back like they were a mere week ago.

Bud stopped. He was making himself miserable with all this thinking.

He picked up his cell phone and dialed Cal.

"Deputy Murphy here," Cal answered.

"Cal, it's Bud. I'm taking the rest of the day off. Who's on duty?"

"I'm on the rest of today, and Hans is on night shift."

"OK, I need to get warmed back up, I think I depleted all my energies yesterday. The Minot Marauders are staying in a condo out by the golf course, so things should be quiet."

"Sounds good. We can handle it. Take care of yourself."

"Thanks, Cal."

Bud hung up, then dialed Wilma Jean.

"Hon, I want to go home for a bit."

"Well, come on home."

"No, I mean Green River. I want to check on things, mow the yard. You going back up with me?"

Wilma Jean paused. "Gee, Hon, Peg and I have plans to go over to Junction today. She really needs to get away. We're going to do a little shopping and go see that new movie, 'Riding in Cars with Dogs.' Speaking of dogs, why don't you take them with you? Actually, take Grid too, so he's not alone."

"I'll starve to death without you," Bud moaned.

"You go down to the Melon Rind. Maureen will fix you up whatever you want—she's a darn good cook," Wilma Jean laughed. "And while you're there, Hon, go check out the bowling alley for me. Krider's girls are running it while I'm gone, and I bet they've made some interesting changes."

Bud groaned. He wanted Wilma Jean to come home. He was tired. All she'd done since they got to Radium was have fun. He felt guilty the minute he thought it, but he wanted her to go home with him.

"OK," he conceded. "I'll come by to get the dogs. You gals have fun. And if I starve to death, you can have my new camera."

Wilma Jean laughed. "I do have plans to get that camera," she said. "You go on home and have a nice relaxing day—you deserve it after all the running around you've been doing, solving crimes. Love you, Hon."

"Likewise," Bud replied, cringing at the thought of all the crimes he'd been running around not solving, Jimmy's murder being one.

CHAPTER 32

Bud stopped and picked up the dogs, who were all excited at being able to go along.

"Don't get any ideas that we're going out on some big adventure, cause we're not, li'l doggies," Bud advised them. "You guys are gonna hang around a nice big shady yard while I mow it." Bud grinned as the dogs jumped into his FJ—all except Pierre, that is, who needed a leg up.

Bud started down Main, then thought of the last time he'd been home and how desultory it had felt. But this was just for the day, he thought, and now he had the dogs with him. But still...

Suddenly, on impulse, he stopped at the Wrangler gas station and ran in, grabbing a sandwich, a cold drink, and some beef jerky sticks for the dogs. He'd go rock hounding instead. That's what he really needed, to be alone and just wander around all day, carefree and enjoying nature.

He headed out north of town, not exactly sure where he was going, but it didn't matter, it was all good. There were hundreds of empty square miles out here, and he knew he was unlikely to meet another soul wherever he went, especially this time of year.

For some reason, he decided to go to Copper Ridge. He hadn't been there for several years, and he used to like to go there when he was younger to look for small azurite nodules that looked exactly like blueberries. He had a whole jar of them back home in Green River.

He finally reached the turnoff, an old dirt road that was partially overgrown with tumbleweeds. It switchbacked up and over the ridge to the Copper Ridge Copper Mine, which had been abandoned for probably a good 50 years.

His FJ had no trouble climbing the steep rocky road—Bud didn't even have to put it in compound gear. The dogs were now excited, heads hanging out the windows, watching for rabbits and rock squirrels. Apparently Bud had lied to them about the adventure thing.

It didn't take long until Bud was at the old mine, which had been reclaimed and closed over. Old mining junk still surrounded it in various stages of rust and disrepair. He parked the FJ, and the dogs tumbled out, excited. They were soon running all around, sniffing.

Bud headed out beyond the mine a bit, hoping to find some new territory for blueberries. The area had been picked over through the years, and he hoped that by getting a bit further out, his chances of finding some would be better.

Like malachite, azurite was a good surface indicator of weathered copper sulfide ores. The blueberries were typically weathered, losing the deep blue color of buried azurite and instead being a pale blue, which made them easy to spot. Bud wandered around, eyes to the ground, finding several, keeping an eye on the dogs, who were now chasing each other, playing with a stick.

He turned, looking out to the skyline. Yesterday's early autumn storm was long gone, and it had warmed up nicely, melting what little bit of snow had fallen here in the lower country. The views here from the ridge were stupendous, and he could see clear to the Bookcliffs above Green River in one direction, and to the Salt Mountains in the other. The Salts had a new mantle of white snow that glistened in the sun.

Bud studied Slickrock Flats in the distance, just below the mesa where Jack and Melba Pilling's ranch set. The domes and fins caught the afternoon sun, which turned them a bright orange. He tried to find the Arrowhead, but it was too distant and blended in with the extensive mass of eroded Navajo sandstone.

He thought again of his failure to make any progress on the Ottin case. Jack had confessed, but somehow Bud knew there was more going on. How could anyone make any sense out of all that, how wondered. He was glad to be away from it. Getting out here was the best thing he could've done, far away from the stress and pressures of being sheriff. He'd always loved rockhounding, it soothed the soul.

Now he had wandered a bit back to where a small cliff crossed, and he turned, following along its face. He'd kind of forgotten all about finding blueberries and was now enjoying watching the dogs run and chase and poke their noses into ground-squirrel holes. A raven flew over, checking them out, and the dogs gave chase, but soon gave up, panting. They were having a ball.

Bud walked out a bit further, thinking it was time to go back and eat that sandwich and give the dogs some water, when he nearly stumbled into a gaping hole. He stopped on its edge, nearly losing his balance.

The hole was about seven feet long by four feet wide, and had definitely been dug by someone, he mused, as opposed to being eroded out, as the dirt from it sat in a nearby pile. He stood there, wondering who would be digging up here—he'd seen similar holes out in dino-bone country where people had been illegally digging for bone, but this was up in the Dakota Formation, and there wasn't much up here in way of fossils.

He jumped down into the hole to examine it closer. It was dug in a layer of whitish-gray sand that looked like blow-sand. The Dakota Formation was millions of years old, but this blow-sand had accumulated much more recently. The hole was over Bud's head, and he was a good six feet tall. Whoever had dug it was dedicated to finding something, as it was a good-sized hole—and it looked to have been dug by hand, as he could see the shovel marks. It must've taken some time to dig a hole like this, he thought.

But what Bud now saw made the hair on his neck stand up. The bottom several feet of sand were a deep green. Bud dug around a bit with his hands, verifying that the layer of sand indeed stretched laterally beyond the hole. It was a continuous layer, and Bud knew what that green was— malachite!

He was standing in the grave of the Malachites.

• • •

Bud was now out of the hole, looking around for clues, his search for azurite blueberries forgotten. Who had done the digging? Whoever it was, it had been several weeks ago, and their footprints had blown away, long gone.

He wandered back over towards the FJ, looking for vehicle tracks, not really expecting to find any. But to his surprise, Bud found what looked like the wind-blown remnants of a track. It had come up the road and on past the mine, making a trail over towards the cliffs where he'd found the grave. Unable to get all the way back there, it had stopped and backed up to a small mound.

A natural loading ramp, Bud thought. A place to drag the skeletons into the pickup—skeletons weren't exactly lightweight, even though one would think they would be. The vehicle had then turned around and headed back out the way it had come, crushing a few rabbitbrush and black-brush shrubs as it went.

Bud stood there, thinking, then suddenly he knew—a Willy's Jeep pickup had narrow tires like that, and Jimmy Ottin had a Willy's pickup. This was definitely where Jimmy had found the Malachites. How he found them, Bud had no idea, but he'd dug them up and loaded them into his pickup, taking them out to the Slickrock Cafe with an ATV.

Bud walked back to the FJ, putting out a pan of water for the dogs, then handing them each a jerky stick. As he sat there, eating his sandwich and drinking a root beer, he flashed back on his dream. He could still hear the voices of the Malachites, telling him they were tired and just wanted to go home. Come to think of it, maybe that's what had brought him here, some hunch, since Copper Ridge was one of the few places around Radium where malachite was found.

What had he been thinking, taking off like this? He had to get back out to the Slickrock Cafe before something happened, before someone decided to move the Malachites.

He called Hoppie and Grid into the FJ, loaded Pierre, then headed back down the steep hill.

CHAPTER 33

Bud had dropped the dogs off at Peg's house and now parked his FJ at the base of the Arrowhead. He had a warm jacket, flashlight, gloves, and a wool hat. He was prepared this time, even though it was warm. The sun was out and the last bits of snow were melting off the crests of the big fins, leaving streaks down the sides. As he passed the campground, he'd noticed it was still empty. The Minot Marauders must still be down at the condo.

He started hiking down the old stock trail, looking for tracks of anyone who might have preceded him. The sand was smooth and wet from the winds and rain of the previous day, and he saw nothing. The firm sand made the going much easier, and he was soon at the Porky Tree.

He now veered off the trail and onto the slickrock, going from fin to fin and tree to tree. He didn't want anyone seeing him, especially none of the regular customers of the Cafe, who he now suspected to be Sonny and Tommy.

It was now late afternoon, and the sun angled down, the air cooling a bit. He didn't have a long time before the sun would set, the fins were already blocking the light and the shade, making the day seem shorter. He wasn't too worried about the Black Beast at this point, but he didn't want anyone to spot him coming.

He angled around the same way he and Krider had come, then changed his mind. If he went up on top, he could see if there were anyone around, but he'd have to come all the way back down and around to get into the Cafe. He didn't want to do that—sunset wasn't that far away, and he wanted to go into the alcove and make sure the Malachites were still there. Someone may have already taken them.

Instead, Bud crept towards the gate of the natural corral, hiding behind rocks, until he was near the Cafe. The rope gate was closed even though the llama was gone. In its place sat a side-by-side ATV.

Just then, he heard hoofbeats coming. He pushed himself back into a thick stand of wavy-leaf oak and held his breath.

It was Patches, but he didn't recognize the rider. He did know it wasn't Jack Pilling—Jack was still in the hospital, plus this rider was too small. Had someone stolen the horse? Whoever it was, they were riding an English saddle and had knee-high leather boots over what looked to be light gray jodhpur pants. A long jacket hung almost to their knees, and they wore a fur-lined winter hat that covered their cheeks, forehead, and most of their face. Bud now noticed a rifle balanced across the rider's lap.

The rider stopped and unlatched the gate rope, rode through, then re-latched it, never leaving the saddle. Whoever it was, they were a seasoned rider, Bud thought.

Now they trotted over to the alcove and stopped, raising the rifle to their shoulder. They made no sound, just sat there on Patches, silently, rifle up, ready to shoot. Finally, he heard something that sounded like, "Come on out."

Bud held his breath. He had no idea what was about to transpire, but he knew it was something important. He took his Ruger from its shoulder holster.

Finally, after what seemed like forever, a man emerged from the alcove. He stepped into full view, and Bud could see he was towheaded, his hair so blonde it was nearly white. It had to be either Sonny or Tommy Ottin, he thought.

He now heard the rider say something, but their back was to him, and he couldn't make out the voice or what they said—but he could make out the voice that answered, and it was definitely that of Sonny Ottin.

"Go ahead and shoot. I don't deserve to walk this planet. A man who would kill his own father shouldn't be allowed to live."

Bud caught his breath. Sonny killed Jimmy? He had never really suspected Sonny of killing his dad. Maybe gambling and grave-digging, but he'd grown up with Sonny and would never have guessed he could kill Jimmy. Sure, the two had sometimes been like oil and water, but he knew Sonny loved his dad deep inside. Bud felt his heart sink. But how did Sonny get Jack's rifle? And why had Jack said he'd done it?

The rider continued to hold the rifle on Sonny, saying something that Bud couldn't make out.

Sonny answered, "I'll tell you. I found out what he was doing here, and I got mad, and you know how my dad could be, totally unreasonable. We were up by the pinion tree. I've never seen him so mad, and we argued big time. I knew he was going to shoot me. He went for his gun, and I hit him on the head with a rock I had in my pocket, a big chunk of malachite. That's how I did it. I killed him. Now do us all a favor and just shoot."

Bud watched intently, but instead of shooting, the rider dismounted, rifle still in hand, dropped Patches' reins, and walked towards Sonny, rifle pointed at the ground.

Now the rider no longer had their back to Bud.

"Sonny," the voice said, "Don't think for a minute you killed your dad, because you didn't. You merely knocked him out."

Bud could now clearly make out the voice.

"I'm the one who killed him. I shot him in the back."

It was Melba Pilling.

● ● ●

Sonny sat down on a nearby rock, a look of shock on his face. Bud still hid, silent, betting that Sonny's look matched the one on his own face.

Melba now put the rifle down, then took off her hat, her gray hair spilling out.

"Jack and I were out riding, looking for a couple of steers that we'd missed in the roundup. I was behind him on Patches—we only have Patches, so when we'd find a steer, I'd jump off and haze it by hand. We came upon your dad. He was out cold."

She continued, "Jack got off Patches, and I slipped over the cantle into the saddle and grabbed the reins. Jack then bent down over Jimmy to see what was going on. Just about then, Jimmy started waking up, moaning. He saw Jack and went for a pistol he had in his pocket. He fired it straight at Jack, barely missing his head. The bullet went into a pinion tree. Jack kind of fell back, shocked. He was trying to help Jimmy, and we talked a lot about it later, and we think Jimmy thought Jack was the one who had hit him and that he was coming after him again. He must've been disoriented. It's the only explanation."

"I panicked. I didn't know what to do. I pulled Jack's rifle from its scabbard, and while doing so, I managed to grab it by the trigger—I had never even held it before, I know nothing about guns. Just as I got the rifle free, it went off. It shot Jimmy in the back just as he shot at Jack the second time, but Jimmy fell over and the shot went wild. Otherwise Jack would be dead right now, I know it."

Melba continued, her voice now soft, and Bud had to strain to hear her.

"I got off Patches, and we could see that Jimmy was hurt pretty bad. Jack took off on Patches for help. He told me later that he'd hoped to see someone on the road but didn't, and ended up going towards the ranch where he could use our phone. But he then heard sirens coming in the distance, so he figured I'd somehow managed to get a cell signal and call for help."

"But I hadn't called anyone at all. I just sat there with Jimmy, trying to stop the bleeding and telling him how sorry I was. He passed away in my arms, Sonny, but the last words he said was to tell you he loved you. I would've told you, but I was afraid I'd go to jail."

Melba now wiped her eyes. "Just then, I also heard the sirens, and I panicked. I've never shot nobody, not even an animal. I took off on foot and angled around and then made my way back to the road, up above the Arrowhead. Jack had turned around and was now riding back down the road, intending to go back to where Jimmy was and get me, tell everyone what happened. We met, and I got on back of Patches. I begged him not to go back down there. I was afraid I'd go to prison, Sonny. I was scared to death."

Bud was now thinking. The hiker that found Jimmy must've found him after Sonny knocked him out and before Melba shot him. The hiker had called the sheriff, thus the sirens and everything. Jimmy had still been alive when the hiker came by.

Now Melba added, "I hope you can forgive me, Sonny." She stood. "But now I think it's time we go find Bud Shumway and tell him everything."

Bud kept his hands in his coat pockets, gun ready just in case, then stepped out from the bushes.

"No need to get the sheriff, Melba, he already knows all about it," he said dryly.

Now Melba and Sonny both looked shocked. Bud was ready in case Melba went for the rifle, but she just sat back down, her face covered with a look of relief and fear.

"You were hiding, listening in?" she asked.

"I was," Bud replied. "It's a handy technique when you're a lawman, it saves you from having to try to get people to confess."

Melba just sat there, looking desultory. Sonny was now standing, nervously fidgeting.

"It's OK, Sonny, I know what's in the alcove, and I know where they came from."

"You do?" Sonny asked, incredulously. "How in hell do you know that? I don't even know that. I've been wanting to take them back to wherever they came from, get rid of the whole damn thing."

"Your dad got them up on Copper Ridge. I found the grave just today."

"No wonder I couldn't find it," Sonny replied. "I've been up at Little Indian looking all over."

Melba pointed towards the alcove. "What's in there, anyway?"

"Just some dead people," Bud answered. "Long time dead, some old skeletons. Sonny's going to tell us all about them, aren't you?" He looked at Sonny questioningly.

"I will, Bud, but I didn't do anything illegal. I didn't dig these guys up, my dad did. That's why we had the big fight, I was just so mad—I couldn't believe he would do that. He's pulled lots of crazy things, but I never took him for a grave robber. But see, he had cancer, and he was desperately trying to come up with money for treatment. He had no health insurance. So he conjured up this Malachite Men drama and ran with it. He was going to sell them for big bucks."

"I can believe that," Bud replied, sitting down next to Melba. "Sounds just like the Jimmy we knew and loved."

Melba now had her hands over her face and was silently crying.

"Are you going to arrest me, Bud? Jack just got out of the hospital, so I might as well be in jail, keep things interesting." She tried to smile.

"Jack's out? Already?" Bud asked.

"He released himself from the hospital this morning, just walked out. Had a friend drive him home."

Bud put his arm around her shoulders.

"Melba, if I arrest you, it will just be a long drawn out ordeal for you and everyone involved, cost the taxpayers a lot of money, and there's a 100 percent chance the judge will throw it out, but if he doesn't, there's a 100 percent chance a jury would find you innocent. It was an accident."

She began silently sobbing.

"I'm just the Interim Sheriff. When Hum gets back on board I'm gonna let him decide what to do. In any case, you're not gonna get any kind of sentence when the judge hears what happened."

"Not arresting me now might cost you your job, Bud," Melba said, drying her eyes.

"I don't think it would have much effect on driving a tractor around a watermelon field, in all honesty, Melba," Bud replied, squeezing her shoulder. "But now that that's settled, we need to plan a funeral."

"A funeral?" Sonny asked.

"We need to rebury those poor fellows," Bud nodded towards the alcove. "They're tired of all the dramatics. I have more questions for both of you, just to tie some things up in my mind, but not today, it's getting late. Hows about tomorrow, say around noon? Sonny, you bring your ATV back in here, get them ready, then we'll have a funeral procession out to Copper Ridge and reinter them. That OK with you?"

"Fine by me, as long as you don't arrest me for the ATV," Sonny said.

"Not this time. You coming, Melba?" Bud asked.

"Bud, I need to stay home with Jack, he's still not that well," she replied.

"I hope he's OK, Melba. That's fine, we'll talk later."

Melba picked up Patches' reins and swung into the saddle, reached down and opened the rope gate, and rode off up the old stock trail.

"Mind if I ride with you?" Bud asked Sonny.

"My pleasure, Bud," Sonny answered, starting up the ATV.

They drove into the dusk, leaving the rope gate hanging open and the Malachites sleeping, deep in the recesses of the Slickrock Cafe.

CHAPTER 34

Sonny pulled off the highway onto the Copper Ridge Road, the refrigerator box in the back of the Willy's pickup bouncing a bit as he crossed the cattle guard. Bud turned to make sure the box was OK, then rested his arm on the passenger window.

"I can't believe you found the grave," Sonny said, steering the pickup up the steep road. The truck had belonged to his dad, but was now his.

"I can't believe it, either," Bud replied. "Pure happenstance. But Sonny, I've been wondering about this all night. Why was Melba at the alcove, pointing her rifle at you? What was going on?"

Sonny laughed. "I actually don't know for sure. Jack's been coming down to my place every so often and playing poker. He always loses, and Melba called me a week or so ago and told me not to let him play anymore. She said he was sending them to the poorhouse. She said if I didn't listen to her, I'd have hell to pay. She then called me at home again two nights ago, said Jack had been gambling again, and even though he had won for once, brought home $500, she was done with it. So, I assume that's what was going on, even though I'd decided to never let Jack play again. I have no idea where he got that money."

"You're running a gambling deal? There in the store?"

Sonny was no longer laughing. "Dammit, Bud, you know me better than that. I learned a lot from my dad, most of which was how not to do things. It started out just a couple of me and my friends playing poker, nothing illegal about it, then Jack come down, he found out somehow, and he wanted to play. I never let it go above $100, then I'd shut it down."

"Was Hans Rohr involved?"

Sonny looked shocked. "Man, you really must think I'm nuts if you think I'd let a deputy sheriff in on a poker game, especially one as serious as that guy is. What makes you think that?"

"That day I was in the cafe, and he and Jack both gave you money."

Now Sonny was laughing again. "Man, oh man, wait till I tell my wife that the sheriff thinks her bakery orders are gambling money. She'll get a kick out of that one. Hans always orders homemade stuff for his family, once a week like clockwork, bread and donuts and sugar cookies. And Jack was paying me my final wages."

"Your wife's a baker?"

"Yeah, she has a little business at home. I'm always taking people's orders. She's also a weaver, makes coats and scarves and stuff out of llama wool. Say, you think that Krider guy you work for would trade some melons for baked goods?"

"I'm sure he would," Bud replied. "And I bet Wilma Jean would buy them for her cafe, too."

Bud wanted to know more about the llamas, but he and Sonny were now at the mine. He jumped out and directed Sonny to the little ramp he'd found earlier, and they unloaded the box. It was the same box that had been painted green and served as the throne for the Malachites. Bud led the way to the grave, and he and Sonny sat the box down at the grave's edge.

Sonny looked into the hole and whistled. "Wow, look at that green layer. No question where they came from. How my dad found them is beyond me, but as you know, he was good at finding things he shouldn't. Should we bury them in the box?"

"I dunno," Bud answered. "But it would be easier. All that malachite makes them heavy."

Bud slid down into the hole, steadying the box as Sonny slid it in, then climbed back out.

"Some archaeologist is gonna scratch their head when they find 600-year-old skeletons with malachite glued all over them buried in a green Amana refrigerator box," Bud grinned.

"How do you know they're 600 years old?" Sonny asked.

"I found the finger bone of one. The lab carbon dated it."

"The finger bone? Where?"

"Out by the cougar petroglyph. I think a raven dropped it there."

"What petroglyph?"

"The one just like that one over there, but up by the Slickrock Cafe." Bud pointed at a petroglyph on the cliff face just above the grave. He then realized he hadn't noticed it last time he was here.

They walked over and studied it.

"Man, Bud, that looks old, like the real deal," Sonny said. It was the same type stylized cougar head, but this one was faded and weathered with time.

Sonny continued, "Right above the grave. Wouldn't it be crazy if my dad was right about all this? Bud, my dad got these bones and decided to make some money from them. He got a bunch of malachite from the Blue Jay Pit and glued it all over them, making them look like they were made of malachite. The parts that didn't have stones were green, so it looked pretty authentic."

Bud sat down on a rock, listening, thinking of his weird dream.

"My dad was desperate, like I said, he had cancer. So he took the skeletons up to the Slickrock Cafe and set them up, put some battery lights and stuff in there, then got in touch with some of his international contacts and told them he'd found evidence of ancient Incans right here in southeast Utah. That caused a stir, believe me. He called them the Malachite Men and was going to sell them for a hundred-thousand bucks. I couldn't believe it, but he had people interested."

"Looks like maybe he was right," Bud offered.

"Yeah, and he must've seen this petroglyph, cause he was out making ones just like it on the rocks, where he could show them to people. He said he'd found the skeletons in the Slickrock Cafe—he never admitted to digging them up, even when I confronted him with it, he knew he could go to prison. I don't know how many people he had interested, but one guy who wanted them ended up not being able to come up with the money. Some private collector from Japan."

"And after your dad was killed?" Bud asked.

"Well, I decided to go ahead with the plot, as there was a guy from Chicago wanting them. I had no idea where my dad got the skeletons, and I suspected they weren't very legal—but a hundred-thousand dollars! Dad was worried that people would come out to the Cafe and find them, so he conjured up this Black Beast thing and got Tommy to run the equipment, and also did this hokey track on a stick thing. Dad figured he'd have them sold and out of there in a few days. Tommy knew nothing about any of this, just another of my dad's wild schemes. He'd sit up there with binoculars and scare people off."

Bud changed the subject, hoping to catch Sonny off guard.

"Do you know who hit Hum?"

Sonny got quiet. "I have no idea. None of us were even up there when it happened, I swear. We were both in the rock shop."

"So, who was the guy with the llamas?" Bud asked, though he thought he knew.

"Man, that really worried me, that night you came down and I was leading Simba home. We took my wife's llamas up there to add some atmosphere to the plot, but they kept getting out and going home, and she was pretty mad about it. I tried to dress up like a Peruvian."

He continued, "I wanted to shut the whole thing down, but we had this one guy from Chicago interested. He finally came out, and I'll be damned if Tommy didn't scare the bejeebers out of him—he shone that Black Beast down there—and all the guy wanted was to get the hell out of there muy pronto. Never heard from him again. That's when I started looking for the grave up at Little Indian, I just wanted it all over and the skeletons gone. No way was I bringing them down to the rock shop or my house. I was about ready to just go bury them out in the desert somewhere."

"What about that evening when I came up and you followed me out? I was pretty worried about that," Bud asked.

"Followed you out? I have no idea what you're talking about. I do recall coming out late and seeing your truck there at the Arrowhead, but I wasn't following you, though I knew Tommy had just scared someone off. That was the night I was taking Simba home—she kept running off, so I brought Babar back, hoping he'd stick around. I was actually worried about you, but when you came out behind me, followed me down the hill with your lights on, I knew you were OK."

It was all starting to make sense, Bud thought. But he had one more question.

"Did you plant a big bullsnake at the bikers' camp?"

Sonny grinned. "I did. That was really stupid, but we had one down at the house, it kept coming into the chicken coop and getting eggs. So I took it up there. I was gonna transplant it anyway, and I was worried those biker guys would go out hiking and find the Cafe, and I was hoping they'd leave. Sounds like they found the snake, huh?"

"It made a local hero out of me when I caught it," Bud replied, smiling. "But Sonny, we have a funeral to get on with, shall we?"

They walked back over to the grave.

"Ashes to ashes, dust to dust..." Bud and Sonny shoveled dirt into the hole, burying the Malachites.

"Man, there's a small fortune in malachite in that hole," Sonny remarked, leaning on his shovel.

"I hope I never see those two again," Bud commented. "And I hope the one doesn't mind that his finger bone's gone."

"If my dad hadn't found those guys, he'd still be alive," Sonny added grimly, tossing his shovel into the bed of the Willy's pickup.

With that, they got in and drove back down the hill.

CHAPTER 35

Bud didn't really want to go visit Jack and Melba, as he knew Jack would be even more crotchety than usual with his head all stitched up, but he had something important to deliver.

He and Krider drove once again up to the wire gate, opening it and going on through. Krider had come down to Radium earlier that afternoon, anxious to hear what had been going on in his absence.

They got out of the sheriff's truck, noticing that Jack's truck and the green car were both there, then knocked on the door. Melba answered, and she looked unsettled to see them, especially when she noticed Bud was carrying a rifle. Bud suspected she still didn't believe he wasn't going to arrest her.

"Come on in, fellas," she said. "Jack's resting, do you want me to get him up?" The two old dogs slept in front of the fireplace, obviously part-deaf to not notice they had company.

"No, it's OK, Melba," Bud answered. "We don't need him. Let him rest. Here's his rifle back, just like I promised. I said I would only keep it a few days. Make sure he gets that safety latch fixed."

Melba looked surprised, then took it and put it in the gun safe.

"He'll be glad to see that," she said. "You boys want some coffee and cookies?" She seemed to relax a bit.

"Not today, we can't stay but a minute. I want to ask you a few questions, if you don't mind."

"You changed your mind, didn't you?" Melba asked, her face drawn.

"No, Melba, I didn't change my mind. If I had, I would need the gun for evidence, wouldn't I?" Bud asked. "If Hum wants it, he'll come and get it, but my hunch is that he won't need it."

"I hope not," Melba answered. "OK, go ahead with the questions. I'll do my best."

"First," Bud asked, "What were you planning to do to Sonny there at the alcove? You had a gun pointed in his general direction."

A rush of blood turned her face red. "It wasn't even loaded. Jack never leaves a loaded gun around, and I don't know how to load one. I was just so sick of him helping Jack gamble our little bit of money away. I wanted him to know I was serious, though there was really nothing I could do."

"But Jack came home with $500."

"I know, but that was a first."

"And he didn't tell you where he got it?"

"He said he won it playing Russian Roulette. That was why I was so mad at Sonny. Things were going too far."

"Well, Melba, first of all, he wasn't with Sonny. He was with the Minot Marauders, a biker gang. I'll let him tell you about it sometime."

Melba gasped. "A motorcycle gang? Oh my God!"

"It's not what you think, Melba. Their leader is the one who saved Jack's life. But anyway, what I really want to know is why you and Jack followed Krider here back to Green River?"

"What? We never followed him, we followed you...oh, so that's what happened. We wondered where you went when he got out. Jack thought it was a dirty trick, but I was glad. Look, Bud, Jack was pretty darn mad when you took his rifle, because he knew it would implicate him in the crime. And he's a good man, he would never tell the truth."

"He's a good man because he lies?"

"In this case, yes, because he would've taken the blame for what I did. So, he wanted to find you and get the rifle back. I went along only to keep him from doing something he shouldn't. He worried me."

"What was he going to do?"

"I don't know, that's why I went along. You know, he seems to be getting more worried about money as time goes on. You saw him, he'd go down to Slickrock Flats in his truck or on Patches just looking for trouble. He's getting more and more cantankerous, and I know he's been worrying about his past catching up to him."

"What in heck is that all about, anyway?"

"I don't know. He has this brother in Texas who's been trying to get ahold of him, and all I know is Jack thinks maybe it has to do with his parents being in debt. They passed away, and ever since then, his brother's been trying to find him. I told Jack that maybe he was in for an inheritance, but he said his dad was so mad at him for dropping out of school he wouldn't even talk to him, so leaving him money was pretty unlikely."

"I might as well show you this, Melba."

With that, Bud took a folded piece of paper from his pocket and handed it to her.

Melba carefully unfolded it, looking suspicious, then started reading it. She looked incredulous.

"How did they find us?" she asked.

"Through the internet. They had an automatic search set up, and when Jack entered the hospital, the newspaper reported his admission, and the search found it."

Melba looked even more incredulous. "They can do that? And now they know where we are?"

"The town only," Bud responded, "not your actual address. They emailed me, wanting that information, but as you can see, I'm not giving it out until I have your permission. Actually, I'm going to let you follow through on all this."

Melba sank into the couch.

"Melba, you should keep reading," Bud offered.

She continued, then sighed.

"I can't believe this, I just can't believe it. You don't think it's a scam of some kind, do you?"

"No, I actually talked to them on the phone. It's quite real."

"What do I need to do now?"

"I would guess call Jack's brother."

"I think I'm gonna pass out," Melba said.

"We have to run, Melba, take good care of Jack."

Melba just sat there, vacantly staring at the wall, then managed to say a faint "Goodbye," not even showing them to the door.

• • •

"What was that all about?" Krider asked once they got outside.

"Jack's brother has been trying to find him for a long time. Jack just inherited a small fortune."

"Whoooeeee!" Krider laughed. "I bet Melba keeps a tight watch on that. No way Jack's gonna gamble that away. And I bet she doesn't leave him after all."

"Yeah, I would guess not. He'll have some money now and won't have to worry, but I bet he's just as crotchety as ever," Bud grinned.

"Wow, big day for them. Let's go on back to the office," Krider replied. "Time to turn in my gun, as I won't be needing it anymore. I think my job is over, and I can get back to writing. I was a deputy for what, about a week? I have a lot more gray hair, but it was quite an experience."

"Prof, we're not done yet," Bud replied.

"We're not?"

"No, we still have to find whoever hit Hum on the head—and why."

"You're right," Krider sighed, as they drove down the road, the fins and domes of slickrock glowing like melted butter in the late afternoon sun.

Bud and Krider soon passed the campground, noting that it was now empty. The tents were gone, and everything had been tidied up, the picnic tables put back in a row. Bud felt a tinge of nostalgia. He knew that things were winding down.

"Never thought I'd see the day I hated to see a biker gang leave the county," he told Krider.

"They weren't a bad bunch, even though they wanted to make you think they were," Krider replied. "I wonder where they're going now?"

Just then, as if on cue, Bud's phone rang. He could see from the caller ID that it was the Emery County Sheriff.

"Barry told me Green River..." he nodded to Krider, then said, "Yell-ow."

"Sheriff, Howie here. I'm out here driving down the highway, and I was just passed by a gang of motorcyclists."

Bud waited. Howie said nothing, so Bud finally asked, "And?"

"Glad you asked. They're all speeding, and I need to pull them over, but I need advice on how to do it when it's just one sheriff up against a whole gang."

"Well, by now, it's probably too late to pull them over, wouldn't you think?"

"No, I can still see them, and now they're cruising up and down Main in town."

"Did they slow down any?"

"Well, it's hard to tell, but maybe so. I guess I could just forget it, that would be one way to stay outta trouble."

"You caught up to them yet?"

"Yeah. They're stopped at the Eastwinds, getting gas."

"Can you see who they are?"

"Yeah, wait a minute...oh dang, it's them Minot Marauders, Bud. They're the ones supposed to be bad news, just came from down your way. What should I do?"

"Well, maybe they're just passing through town."

"I sure hope so."

Bud continued, "I heard they were sometimes called the Devil's Minions and Spawn of Satan. Say, Howie, if they stick around, here's what you do. You pull their leader over—he's the one wearing the red bandanna. You tell him they've been speeding, but instead of fining them, you want them to all do community service. And when he asks what that would be exactly, you tell him they have to ride in the parade tomorrow. That's their fine."

"Ride in the parade? Here in Green River?"

"Yeah, and if Larry Digham protests, you tell him he's obstructing justice, cause you just fined them that for community service."

"Oh, I know he'll protest. I'm just gonna hope they pass on through."

"OK, and you tell the leader, his name is Barry, that Sheriff Bud Shumway's gonna be there to see that parade."

"Oh jeezlouise, Bud, that's great. You guys are coming up, then? I'm gonna drive the tractor with the Krider girls' float. Larry said it was OK. Maureen's gonna ride in a big green and red convertible—she's the Melon Queen. She made herself a green and red dress and she'll wear a big green crown."

"I wouldn't miss it for anything," Bud replied.

CHAPTER 36

Bud and Krider pulled into the drive at Peggy Sue's. Once again, the street was full of vehicles, and they could hear loud voices coming from the house in what sounded like a big party, dogs barking and people whooping and hollering.

Bud looked at Krider, then said, "I'm thinking maybe Hum came home."

Sure enough, when they got into the house, there sat Hum in his big lounger chair, feet kicked back and people fawning over him, asking questions like, "Could you hear people talking around you?" and, "Did you see a tunnel with a white light at the end when you got knocked out?"

Hum seemed to be enjoying the attention, but he also looked tired.

"How long's he been out of the hospital?" Bud asked Peggy Sue.

"Only an hour, and I'm gonna run everyone off, cause he's looking tired."

Bud went over to Hum, putting his hand on Hum's shoulder and squeezing it. Hum jumped a bit until he saw who it was, then grinned. Bud then leaned down and whispered in Hum's ear, "Hum, Wilma Jean's making me get my other ear pierced."

Hum, who had previously been rather quiet, let out a guffaw, then grabbed Bud by the arm.

"Bud Shumway, you rascal! I owe you a bunch."

"I kind of liked it better when you couldn't talk," Bud teased.

"Yeah, job security for you, eh?" Hum laughed.

Peggy Sue was now shushing everyone out, saying Hum needed to rest. The room was soon quiet.

Krider sat down by Hum. Wilma Jean brought everyone hot chocolate and warm banana bread, then asked Bud if she could talk to him in the kitchen. He ambled back and leaned against the cupboard.

"Hon, me and Peggy Sue are gonna take off for town to check out that new antique shop, but first I want to give you a little present I got in Junction. Everything's just so hectic, and I want you to have it before we go to the parade, so you can use it."

She handed Bud a small box. It read "Junction Jewelers."

Bud was pretty sure he didn't want whatever was in that box, but he didn't have the heart to tell Wilma Jean, so he opened it.

Sure enough, it was a new ear-post, but this one had a small malachite stone on it. He tried to smile.

"Gee, thanks, Hon, it's really pretty."

Wilma Jean started laughing.

"You're a good sport." She took the box away.

"That's really for me, I've got the mate in my pocket. Here's your real gift."

She took a medium-sized box from where it was hid behind the cookie jar.

Bud opened it, not daring to hope. Sure enough, it was a Canon digital SLR camera, complete with several lenses.

"I can't believe my eyes," he grinned, then hugged Wilma Jean.

"Now you have to give me back the other camera," she said. "I got it for myself but let you use it until I could get yours. It matches the color of my Lincoln."

Bud took the pink camera from his pocket and handed it to her, hugging her again.

She added, "Hon, I gotta admit, me and Peg went kind of wild in Junction."

"What did you do?"

With that, Wilma Jean pulled her shirt over just enough that Bud could see—there, on her left shoulder, was a small red and green tattoo—of a watermelon.

Bud wasn't sure what to say, so he just grinned and hugged her again.

"And Hon," she continued. "I'm about ready to go home. It's been fun, but I miss Green River."

Bud grinned, hugged her yet again, then went back into the living room and sat down. Before long, they'd be getting themselves big Harleys, he figured, to go with the piercings and the tattoos.

He sat there for a minute, then collected himself. He wanted to tell Hum all about Jimmy and what had transpired, but he wasn't sure Hum was still awake, the way he was leaned back in his chair.

Bud said, "Hum, we figured it all out, and I can tell you about it later, cause you need to rest. This is Bill Krider, the guy I'm working for up in Green River."

Hum opened his eyes and nodded at Bill.

"Hum, we're going back up there tomorrow for a couple of days, but I'm going to hold down the fort here for you until you get back on the job. It shouldn't be too long. Bill and I are going to leave you alone here in a minute so you can rest, but I have to tell you one thing. We figured out who killed Jimmy and all that, but we still haven't figured out who hit you on the head. Maybe when you get some rest you'll want to tell us what you remember."

Hum sat up, shaking his head.

"Bud," he said, "I could hear you talking about that every damn time you came into my room, and I always wanted to tell you, but I couldn't talk. The truth is, I didn't get hit, I slipped on that damn ledge and fell—I know, a seasoned outdoorsman like me, but that's exactly what happened. Anyway, excuse me, but I'm gonna take a nap now."

Bud grinned, looking at Krider.

Krider said, "That's the kind of mystery ending I like— short and sweet. And you know, I'm hungry. I never did get anything to eat at that darn Slickrock Cafe. Not even a cup of coffee."

"Let's go turn in your gun and then get something at the Uranium Cafe," Bud replied.

They both walked out the door and on to better things.

About the Author

Chinle Miller writes from southeastern Utah, where she spends most of her time wandering with her dogs. She has a B.A. in Anthropology and an M.A. in Linguistics and is currently working on a degree in geology.

If you enjoyed this book, you'll also enjoy the first book in the Bud Shumway mystery series, *The Ghost Rock Cafe*. And don't miss *Desert Rats: Adventures in the American Outback* and *Uranium Daughter*, both by Chinle Miller.

And if you enjoy Bigfoot stories, you'll love *Rusty Wilson's Bigfoot Campfire Stories* and his many other Bigfoot books, available in paperback or as ebooks from yellowcatbooks.com and your favorite online retailer.

You can also find unique Bigfoot hats and apparel at yellowcatbooks.com.

CPSIA information can be obtained at www.ICGtesting.com
Printed in the USA
LVOW08s2227150215

427162LV00024B/551/P